A huge dark shape materialized out of the mist

Liv's mouth gaped open. In front of her stood a great black horse, ridden by an imposing figure, wrapped in some kind of a cloak, half-hidden by darkness. Gasping for breath, Liv hugged her arms to her chest as the horse danced impatiently beside her.

"You shouldn't be out here, alone at night. It could be dangerous." The stranger's voice, disembodied, floated eerily on the dark, misty night.

Liv swallowed hard and tried to make sense out of what was happening. She couldn't see the man's face, but his voice sounded strange, the accent more British than American, and the words he spoke could have been a warning— or a threat.

"Do you want a ride or not?" the horseman said impatiently. "Decide, woman. I must be off."

Liv weighed her options. If she refused his offer, she might be stuck here all night. And after all, hadn't she just been telling herself she needed a little adventure? With a spirit of daring that surprised her, Liv took the stranger's hand and was swung up into the saddle behind him.

Dear Reader,

When our book, *The Pirate's Woman*, was published in January 1994, we held our breaths. Would Temptation readers accept a magical tale of a twentieth-century heroine and an eighteenth-century rogue? Happily, the book was very successful, not only in North America, but all over the world.

We then brought our editors an idea for a new miniseries: exciting heroes traveling across time and meeting wonderful, contemporary heroines. Everyone was enthusiastic and thus, ROGUES was born.

For our contribution, we chose another swashbuckling hero from the eighteenth century—the Highwayman. What woman wouldn't be swept away by a dark, romantic figure, riding through the night atop his great black steed, his cape blowing behind him in the wind? Our heroine, Olivia, is captivated from the moment she encounters Gabriel Stratton, Baron Northcliffe and suspected "Highwayman of Haroldsgate." Their story is filled with passion, humor and spine-tingling adventure as they battle the evil around them and their ever-present enemy, time.

We hope *The Highwayman* will sweep you away into a land of fantasy and romance where the impossible can happen and true love conquers all.

Enjoy!

Madeline Harper

a.k.a. Shannon Harper and Madeline Porter

THE HIGHWAYMAN
Madeline Harper

Harlequin Books

TORONTO • NEW YORK • LONDON
AMSTERDAM • PARIS • SYDNEY • HAMBURG
STOCKHOLM • ATHENS • TOKYO • MILAN
MADRID • WARSAW • BUDAPEST • AUCKLAND

To Susan Sopcek, as always, for her support,
and to Brenda Chin for her enthusiasm.
Special thanks to C.B. of Copake for her hospitality
in New York State.

ISBN 0-373-25701-5

THE HIGHWAYMAN

ROGUES

ROGUES ACROSS TIME

THE HIGHWAYMAN

During the seventeenth and eighteenth centuries, daring robbers called "Highwaymen" roamed the thoroughfares of England. Armed only with pistols and their own audacity, they waylaid travelers, relieving them of gold and jewelry…and sometimes even stealing a lady's heart. These rogues became romantic figures, and soon the legend of "the Highwayman" grew in story and song.

Gabriel Stratton, Baron Northcliffe, was well-known for racing across the English countryside in the dark of night, mounted upon his great black stallion, Eclipse. The townspeople feared him, and the gentry shunned him, for it was rumored that the baron was the notorious "Highwayman of Haroldsgate." Even though he denied that charge, as well as others brought against him by his enemies, he was arrested by the High Sheriff and hanged for his crimes in the year 1796.

1

"SELL IT, Liv. You'd be foolish not to. Besides, I'd like to have the listing for my real estate agency!"

Olivia Johnson shook her head thoughtfully. "Not so fast, Peggy. I haven't made up my mind yet."

"What in the world are you going to do with a defunct *horse farm?*"

Liv closed the door to her grandparents' house firmly behind her. "I don't know. But it's not easy to give up a home that has been in the family for generations."

"You certainly don't plan to *live* here." Peggy's plump face took on a look of mock incredulity. "Do you?"

Liv smiled at the real estate agent's remark. "You make country living sound like a jail sentence, Peggy."

"That's exactly what it would be for you. Honey, I've known you for years and I understand how hard you've worked to get where you are. Your flair, your whole lifestyle would be wasted here."

"Maybe," Liv answered. "But it's only a three-hour commute from New York City, and I could use one floor of the farmhouse as a studio. It would be a perfect place to design my jewelry."

"Good Lord!" Peggy exclaimed. "You're not kidding. Stop and think, Liv. You'd be stuck way out here in the country, alone. It would never work."

Liv met the older woman's eyes squarely. "I *am* thinking, but I haven't made up my mind about anything yet. Except that I need to get back to the inn before dark." She took the agent's arm and steered her toward their cars parked under the shadow of a giant oak.

"You're at the Boot and Bottle?" Peggy said. "Quaint little place. Almost like an old tavern in the English countryside, not a converted hotel in upstate New York."

"It's comfortable," Liv acknowledged. And a little too quaint for my tastes, she thought, but didn't dare admit. She didn't want to give Peggy any more ammunition. Not when she had begun to think seriously about relocating.

"It's more comfortable than this house, which you couldn't possibly live in," Peggy added. "And I doubt if your boyfriend would come with you."

"What boyfriend?" Liv asked.

"Well, I just assumed—"

"No more." Liv answered quickly. Then she let out a sigh. People assumed a lot about her. And why not? She'd been responsible for projecting the image of a carefully crafted life of sophistication that would certainly include men. In fact, she had been in a serious relationship for a couple of years, but when he'd decided to move to Phoenix, Liv had opted to stay in New York. They weren't surprised to find the long-distance love affair didn't work, and the final break had been easy.

She walked along beside the older woman, her feet making crunching noises in the dried mud. Olivia

Johnson, the epitome of chic, very different from the insecure young girl who had spent vacations on her grandparents' farm. Today, success was hers. In New York City, she had a select group of close friends and many acquaintances; she ate in all the best restaurants and saw all the new shows. Over the years, she'd worked hard to build and maintain her image as a fashionable Manhattan career woman. But the strain was getting to her. She had begun to resent the rigid role she'd created for herself and longed for something else. Maybe a change in life-style was just what she needed.

"I've lived in New York City a long time, Peggy," she said as they reached their cars. "But I still don't feel at home there. This is home, this farm."

"Where you've never lived for more than a couple of months and where you couldn't possibly be happy."

"Maybe not. But I can't see selling the farm to someone else. On the other hand, I'm not rich enough to keep my apartment in New York and this place, too," she admitted.

Both women opened their car doors at the same time, and as Liv slid into her seat, Peggy tried one last time.

"Development! That's the way to go. Divide the property into one-acre plots, and the land will sell so fast it'll make your head spin. Not to mention that it'll make you richer than—"

She was still babbling on as Liv gave her a wave and sped away. At the end of the rocky dirt road, she turned left, toward the inn.

"One-acre plots? Not on your life," Liv muttered to herself. Knowing that her grandparents would consider that a desecration of her birthright, she found the idea appalling. But her grandparents had been gone a long time. She *should* be sensible and let Peggy sell the farm. The agent was practically salivating for the listing.

"But look at the setting!" she exclaimed aloud, slowing down to gaze across the acres of rolling meadowland that were only beginning to come alive with the arrival of summer. How could she sell it to strangers? On the other hand, how could she afford to hang on to it without giving up her place in the city?

She had never considered moving to the country an option. And yet the timing seemed right. She had no significant other in her life, no friends she couldn't leave behind, no work that she couldn't do out of the farmhouse, just as she now did out of her Soho loft. Occasional commutes to New York City on business wouldn't be a problem.

Besides, her heart was in the country, Liv thought as a sudden movement caught her attention. She slowed her rental car almost to a stop and watched a pair of deer, a doe and a buck, move from the shelter of the trees to graze on the new grass, picking their way along with breathtaking grace.

She watched for a long quiet moment. The sight of deer was not unfamiliar to her. During her childhood, Liv had spent many school holidays with her grandparents. She remembered going out into the meadow with her grandfather during heavy snows to feed the deer. While other residents strung barbed wire and sprayed chemicals to keep the deer away, her grandfather had spread hay for them along with his horses.

"The deer were here first," he'd told her philosophically.

After a few minutes' thought, Liv turned onto the Highback Road, an alternate route that was longer but far more scenic. At least it would be if the fog that was threatening held off. This road would take her eventually to the little town of Chester.

As she topped a hill and rounded a curve, Liv saw a familiar rambling building. The Magic Carpet bookstore was still there! Without hesitation, she turned in to the graveled parking area and stopped. The funny old shop seemed to go on and on, with haphazard additions spreading out toward untended flower beds. It was exactly the same as she remembered when she was a kid.

Nothing had changed inside, either. There was the familiar smell of old books and fine leather and the warmth of soft light filtering in through dusty windows. And at the front desk, his nose buried in a book, was Mr. Hapgood. As a child, Liv had wondered how many hours the Magic Carpet owner spent reading.

"Hello, Hap," she called out.

He looked up, his forehead creased in a frown.

"It's me, Olivia Johnson."

His face lit up, and he let out a hoot of recognition. "Little Olivia, as I live and breathe. All grown-up."

Hap unwound his lanky frame from the chair and took a couple of steps toward her. "What a surprise." He grabbed her hands, enveloping them in his. "I was sorry to hear about your grandparents, but we all knew Garner wouldn't live long after your grandma died. Those two were so much in love."

"They were special," Liv said, feeling a prick of tears in her eyes. "I've inherited the farm," she told him.

"I heard that." Hap pushed his rimless glasses up on his balding head. "Now, where's your mother these days?"

"Remarried and living in Florida. Widowhood didn't suit her."

"She gave up the diner?"

"Finally." Liv forced a smile. She'd hated the New Jersey town where she grew up, the diner her parents owned and everything about it, including the apartment above where they'd lived in four crowded rooms. Liv had worked as a waitress in the diner every day after school until she'd escaped to college. The only bright spots in her life had been the visits to her grandparents' farm.

"Well, I'm glad to hear your mother's doing well," Hap responded. "And what about you—married yet?"

"Nope. Single and working in New York. I'm a designer for a couple of jewelry companies."

"Fancy ones, I bet." He removed his glasses and examined them closely.

"I have to admit they are."

"And I'm sure you do fine work. You always were an artistic kid, as well as an avid reader. Your grandparents were mighty proud of you. Seems like just yesterday," he said, polishing his glasses and returning them to the top of his head. "But it was a long time ago, I guess."

"It was. I'm twenty-six now. Time flies."

"Don't remind me. But time has been very kind to little Olivia. Turned you into a fine-looking woman.

Now, don't take this unkindly, but even though you were a smart kid, you weren't exactly—"

"I know. I wasn't a great beauty," she finished for him. "More like hopeless. Tall. Skinny. And those awful braces."

"The potential was there. We just were too blind to see it," Hap said. "But I do remember those big blue eyes. They came from your grandma, Katie. Irish through and through and a real beauty herself." He patted Liv's arm. "Thanks for stopping by to let me get a look at you."

"I couldn't pass by the Magic Carpet. I spent a lot of happy hours here, lost in books." She glanced around the main room where used books were stuffed into floor-to-ceiling shelves. "Still in the middle of cataloging?" she teased.

"Nothing's changed," Hap said. "I never seem to get organized, and the cookbooks are still mixed in with the poetry. But you always managed to find your way around."

"And I will again. Right now," she told him. "I'm going to browse for a while. I need something wonderfully distracting to curl up with at the inn tonight."

Just then, the bell tinkled, and two more customers came into the store. As Hap turned to greet them, Liv slipped away, down a step into another level of the shop. She wanted something compelling to read, something that would take her mind off the decision she needed to make about the farm.

She surveyed the room. Books that wouldn't fit into the jammed shelves were piled on tables and on the floor. As Liv ducked around a corner, she caught her heel on the frayed carpet, almost falling. "Damn."

She regained her balance, and a title caught her eye. *Rogues Across Time.* The book teetered precariously on the edge of a shelf. It looked old, with a well-worn brown leather cover. Instinctively, she reached for it. The leather felt warm and inviting. Was it her imagination, or did touching the book send a tingle down her spine? She opened it and scanned the table of contents. The Cowboy. The Pirate. The Outlaw. The Knight. The Highwayman.

Highwayman.

An image flashed into her mind of a dark foggy night. And a man, on a huge black horse, his cape swirling in the wind. She quickly turned the pages, searching for a description of the Highwayman. Suddenly, his likeness was there before her.

Even in the black-and-white reproduction, his was the most handsome face she'd ever seen. His black hair flowed away from a high forehead. His eyes were dark, too, and they stared at her with a mixture of arrogance and invitation. High cheekbones, a straight strong nose and a mouth filled with humor and sensuality.

"Wow!" Liv breathed. She felt her pulse quicken. The Highwayman was everything a storybook lover should be. Dashing. Romantic. The very personification of adventure. His mystique was the opposite of her life at the moment, which was far from adventurous. The highwayman's story would provide what she needed— escape into another world on a foggy night.

She scanned the text and learned that the man in the drawing was known as Baron Northcliffe. He was born in 1768 and died in 1796. She stopped her page-turning, backed up and reread the dates. He was only twenty-eight when he died! True, those eighteenth-century types didn't live long, but such a healthy-looking specimen should have at least made it to thirty-five.

Then she found the explanation. Northcliffe had been hanged in the gallows! Liv looked at the portrait again. It wasn't possible. A man that heroic couldn't have been a criminal.

She had to know more. Clutching the book, she headed for Mr. Hapgood and his antiquated cash register.

A HALF HOUR LATER, Liv found herself in her car, inching forward through the mist which was suddenly heavier. Thick gray tendrils swirled around, obscuring all landmarks. The road, which had seemed familiar to her earlier, was suddenly mysterious and foreboding. She drove on, slowly, unable to recognize any of the landscape. As darkness fell and the fog grew thicker, Liv felt as though she were in a foreign land.

She'd lost time at the Magic Carpet with her purchase of *Rogues Across Time*. There had been no price tag on the book, and Hap's woefully inadequate card-file inventory had shown no record of it ever having been in stock. After musing aloud for ten long minutes about its possible origins and arrival in his store, he'd finally set a price that was very reasonable, considering the book's fine leather binding and high-quality paper. But by then the sun had set and the mist had moved in.

She turned on the windshield wipers, moved the defroster switch to high and ineffectively dabbed with a tissue at the moisture on the car window. She was thinking about pulling over and waiting for the fog to lift, when the mist was blown aside by a guest of wind. In the brief moment when visibility improved, Liv saw a sign pointing toward Chester. She didn't recall the road. But that meant nothing; a lot of time had passed since she'd last driven the county's back roads. She preferred to trust the signs over her memory and made a quick turn—just as the fog rolled back in like an enormous dark cloud, obscuring everything.

Relying on her memory of what she'd seen in those few brief clear moments, Liv kept going, holding the steering wheel steady in her attempt to complete the turn.

A jolting thud told her she wasn't going to make it. She stepped on the brake, but it was too late. The car spun on the damp road, tilted alarmingly and crashed into a ditch. Despite her seat belt, Liv was hurled forward into the windshield, and everything went black.

GROANING, Liv opened her eyes and strained to see into the darkness. Her head hurt like hell, but as she moved her arms and legs, she discovered that nothing was broken. Well, that was something to be thankful for, Liv thought. But there wasn't much else. She was stuck in a wrecked car, under a blanket of fog, in the middle of nowhere.

"Damn," she said aloud. "What now?"

The car was tilted sideways and the entire driver's side was crushed into the ditch. There was no way she would be able to get out of that door. She looked up. The other door was above her head but obviously undamaged. Liv unhooked her seat belt and crawled up, across the seat, to the passenger side of the car.

Getting out was another matter. She struggled with the door handle, forcing it down. Stopping for a moment, she caught her breath, tried to ignore her splitting headache and pushed with all her might against the door, opening it wide enough to squeeze through.

At last, Liv was outside in the cool night air, sitting on the side of her upturned rental car, considering her next move. She'd have to take a hike toward town, obviously. Trouble was, she didn't have identification, a flashlight or any kind of protection. Leaning over, she poked her head back into the car and tried to get her handbag. But it had been flung—along with the book— onto the floor beneath the steering wheel. She leaned in as far as she dared, but the purse and book were out of her reach.

"Dammit," she cursed under her breath. Then she remembered. There was pepper spray in the glove compartment. As a matter of course, she'd brought it with her from the city. She opened the compartment and rummaged around until she found the aerosol container.

"Armed and ready," Liv said as she slid off the car into the ditch and struggled up the embankment to the road. The fog was thicker than ever, and Liv couldn't see any more than a few feet in any direction. Relief that she was unharmed, except for the bump on her head, mixed in her mind with a healthy dose of anxiety. She had no idea when—or if—another car would come along. Nor did she see any houses in the area. There was nothing around her but darkness and swirling mist.

But she couldn't stay here. She had to take her chances walking toward civilization, which she figured, by process of elimination, lay ahead. There was nothing behind her for miles, except the Magic Carpet. And by now, Hap had probably locked up and gone home.

So she would forge ahead.

That's when she heard the sound, faint at first, muffled by the fog. Unsure of where it came from, she stood in the middle of the road, holding her breath, waiting.

Then she realized that the sound was hoofbeats—coming closer and closer.

"Help! Over here!" Liv shouted as loudly as she could. "I need help!"

The hoofbeats drew nearer, and Liv squinted into the haze. What if the rider didn't see her? She would be trampled!

She shouted again. "I'm here. Slow down. Please!"

A huge dark shape materialized out of the mist, and a black horse appeared with a man astride it, wrapped in some kind of cloak, his face hidden by the darkness.

Liv's mouth gaped open. A horseman in a cape? No! She shook her head to clear it, which only intensified the pain and caused a wave of dizziness to overcome her. Gasping for breath, she hugged her arms to her chest and tried to remain upright as the great black horse danced impatiently beside her and the stranger hovered above.

She took a step back and reached for the pepper spray in her pocket. Just clutching it gave her courage, even though she felt dwarfed and vulnerable beside the shadowy apparition that towered over her.

"I need help," she repeated.

"You should not be out here, alone at night. It could be dangerous." His voice, disembodied, floated eerily on the dark, misty night.

Liv swallowed hard and tried to make sense out of what was happening. She had no idea who this man was, coming out of the fog astride a huge black horse. She couldn't see his face, but his voice sounded strange, the accent more British than American, and the words he spoke could have been a warning—or a threat.

She tried to keep her own voice steady. "I ran off the road in the fog. My car is over there in the ditch. I wonder if you'd mind stopping by the garage in town and asking them to send out a truck—"

"I have no idea what your words mean," the man said, shifting on his horse, which moved nervously beneath him. When he pulled back on the reins, the horse reared up on its hind legs, and Liv gasped, ducking out of the way.

"Watch out!" she cried.

She heard his laughter, low and rumbling. "From your cries, I assume you are in trouble, and yet you back away from me. Do you want to ride or not?"

"No! What I want is for you to send a tow truck to—"

"'Tow truck?'" He pronounced the words as if they were foreign. "No one will come out on a night like this except perhaps your family."

"I have no family here," she told him.

"Then decide, woman. I must be off. Will you be going with me or not?"

Liv weighed her options. If she refused his offer, she might be stuck here all night. And, after all, hadn't she just been telling herself she needed a little adventure. With a spirit of daring that surprised her, Liv decided.

ONLY AFTER she was on the horse, straddling its wide rump, her arms wrapped around the stranger's waist, did she realize she had made the wrong choice.

The animal lunged forward, and she held on for dear life, bumping up and down with a force that jarred her already pounding head. She grasped the man tighter, buried her face in his black cloak and prayed that she would be able to hang on. Even while she clutched him, Liv wondered what in the world had possessed her. It wasn't like her to be impetuous or careless. Or blatantly foolish. Now she was all three.

He wasn't even keeping to the road, she realized as the trees closed in on them, whipping at her face. They were on some kind of narrow, hilly path. She bounced dangerously and then felt the horse give a mighty lunge and take to the air.

They'd jumped a ditch, landing on the opposite bank with such force that she almost slid off. "Damn," she cried, "I'll never survive this."

But she did, finally even getting into the rhythm of the horse's gait, not resisting but moving with the animal.

Still, it was madness. She couldn't believe that she was riding through the night on a huge horse behind a complete stranger. It must be the shock of the accident, she decided—or maybe she was dreaming. That could be the only explanation for her unlikely behavior.

But the wind in her face was certainly real enough and so was the fabric of the cape pressed against her cheek, not to mention the muscular body of the man wearing it.

Who was he, and why in the world was he riding this enormous black horse and wearing a swirling black cape?

Maybe he was part of some deviant cult! Liv berated herself for putting her faith in the unknown. If she'd only stayed in the car, none of this would have happened. The rider, whoever he was, probably wouldn't have noticed the wreck in the ditch when he galloped by. True, that would have meant staying all night huddled alone in the dark. But so what? She could have managed, and by morning someone would have found her—someone with the sense to call a tow truck.

At least she had the pepper spray. The thought of the can nestled deep in her pocket was reassuring. If worse came to worst she could defend herself, but there didn't seem to be a need for protection from the rider, who had simply swept her up behind him, whirled his mount around and set out across the countryside.

Somehow, along with her discomfort, unease and anxiety, Liv felt a sense of wonder and exhilaration. And freedom. Could anything be more romantic than riding through a misty night with a dark, mysterious stranger?

Her rescuer rode effortlessly. He was one with the horse, galloping down a twisting road. As she allowed her body to flow into his, Liv imagined they were both characters out of a storybook.

The fog writhed around them in long clinging wisps, but they moved as if by magic. Liv's hair came undone, and the pins she'd used to hold it in a smooth chignon at the back of her neck flew away in the wind. She closed her eyes and tightened her hold on the stranger's waist. She wasn't afraid anymore. She felt marvelously alive and wanted to laugh out loud. The situation was unbelievable, preposterous—and somehow totally glorious.

Her tawny hair whipped around her face, and she felt herself being transformed—into another world, another place, blowing through the winds of time.

That was absurd, of course. She realized that as soon as the horseman reined in and they slowed to a walk. Her adventure had ended, and she felt a pang of disappointment. She peered around his broad back and saw the outline of a few buildings, most of them dark, but here and there a dim light shone in a window. If they were in Chester, then where were the street lamps? The store lights?

The horse stopped beneath a weathered sign that creaked eerily in the wind. The Boot and Bottle. Liv let out her breath with a long sigh. She'd made it to the inn!

Clumsily, Liv slid from the horse, her long filmy skirt catching the wind. She fought the fabric down, glancing at the man, but she couldn't see his face. The lights at the front of the inn seemed to have burned out. "Thank you for the ride."

He leaned down from the horse, his face still in shadow. "And what of my payment?"

"I'm sorry. I left my purse in the—"

"A kiss, wench."

Liv laughed. Whoever he was, he was outrageous. "I don't think so, but if my credit is still good, I'll buy you a drink." With those words, she moved out of the wind, pushed open the inn door—and stopped dead in her tracks.

THE INN'S BRIGHT friendly tavern, a quaint replica of an English pub, was now dark and filled with smoke. Sitting at crowded tables was a collection of rough-looking men, wearing wrinkled and unkempt clothing—coarse woven shirts, tattered leather vests, patched trousers and worn boots. A few were sporting wide-brimmed hats, most were smoking foul-smelling pipes.

What in the hell was going on? Where were the polished tables and shiny brass lanterns, the mahogany bar and rows of sparkling glasses? The dart board was gone, and so were the cozy booths. She tried to make sense out of the transformed scene that looked like something from the eighteenth century.

"Shut the door, now, will ye? No use letting in the night air." A short, stout woman garbed in a floor-length cotton dress covered by a stained apron approached Liv. The woman's face was round and full, and in the puffiness her eyes appeared no larger than raisins. Her nose was small, and so was her pursed little mouth.

"'Tis about time ye got here. I been running meself to death, doin' all the servin'."

Liv closed the door. "Are you speaking to me?"

The woman put her hands on her abundant hips. "Who do ye think I be speakin' to, King George the Third? 'Course, I be speakin' to ye, wench."

Liv drew herself up to her full five feet six inches and pushed the windblown hair out of her face. Whoever this woman before her was, she had far less clout than the ill-mannered New York maître d's whom Liv had long ago learned to handle. She could certainly deal with this one the same way.

"I have no idea who you are or what happened to the couple who owns this place," she said. "I assume you have an explanation. And I'd like to hear it."

Her outburst didn't even faze the woman. Obviously what worked in New York City didn't work in Chester, or at least not in the strange place the inn had become.

"I don't know what nonsense ye be talkin'," the woman said. "I do know ye'll work here this night." She looked Liv up and down with her little round eyes. "Me brother promised to send over a sturdy servin' wench from the next village. Ye're tall enough, and that's a fact. Ye don't look that strong to me, but as they say, looks can deceive. What's the answer, missy?"

Serving wench? This odd little woman thought she was a waitress! Liv looked around the room again. All eyes were on her, waiting expectantly. Was this a joke? Why was everyone in the Boot and Bottle in costume?

And then it came to her. A historical re-creation! Of course. The little town of Chester was reliving the past with some kind of town festival. But it did seem peculiar that the young couple who owned the inn hadn't mentioned it to her or that there'd been no posters announcing the occasion.

Wait, she admonished herself. When had she looked around or listened to what was going on at the inn? Too consumed with worry about the farm, she'd paid no attention to anything or anyone. The whole town could have disappeared around her, and she probably wouldn't have noticed.

The situation certainly had her attention now. Liv broke into a smile. "What a clever idea," she said to the stout woman. "I'd love to join in—but just for a short while. I still need to have someone pull my rental car out of the ditch, but it's not going anywhere, and most of the town seems to be here, anyway. I don't have a costume—"

"There be another apron behind the counter. Me husband Simon'll get ye started. Now get a move on."

Liv shook her head in amazement. The woman playing the innkeeper's wife was wonderful, with just the right touch of no-nonsense sharpness. And her accent was perfect, better than anything she'd heard in the movies. A little old-fashioned, as befitted the situation, with a wonderful British rural vocabulary and brogue. She wondered if the woman's role was scripted.

After another sharp command was thrown at her, Liv walked toward the bar, wrinkling her nose at the mixture of odors, including candle smoke, spilled ale—and unwashed bodies. She could have done without the lack of deodorant. It didn't seem necessary to go that far to capture the spirit of the times, but apparently there were no holds barred in this reenactment.

Liv glanced down at her own clothes. She couldn't have fit in better if she'd planned it. Her long cotton paisley skirt hung over the tops of her knee-high leather boots, and her blouse, which she'd bought on a whim, was white with puffy sleeves and an inset of lace at the neckline.

It was just her luck to have been given the role of a serving wench. But God knows, she'd had enough waitressing experience in her life to be believable. She was willing to give it a whirl.

A large muscular man stood behind the bar, drawing mugs of ale with a flourish. Liv flashed him a grin. "I'm the newest volunteer. Looks like fun, but I can't take part for very long."

Simon's gaze was withering. "None of yer lip! The wench we had in here before ye didn't last long. If ye want to better her record, just do the work and heed what Nora says."

Liv rolled her eyes heavenward. She'd never seen people more into their roles—or their accents. Thinking at first that they lived in the area, she was now beginning to believe the town had hired actors.

Simon and Nora, if those were their real names, seemed determined not to break character. She'd play along for a while to be a good sport. Then she'd go to her room and start calling—first the car rental company, then the local garage.

Liv pushed her hair behind her ears, tied on the apron and took a heavy tray from Simon, balancing it carefully. It had been a few years since she'd waited on tables at her parents' diner, but she could still handle a full tray.

"Where do these go?"

"Table in the corner," Simon answered with a shake of his bald head. "And they be thirsty, girl, and tired of waitin'."

Carrying the heavy tray, she threaded her way among the tables. Just as she'd observed when she came into the tavern, there weren't any women. Where were they? Relegated to a quilting bee, making candles, pottery or even weaving for the tourists. Surely the festival would attract an audience. But where *were* the tourists?

Well, it was still early. Maybe the real production didn't begin until later. Or this could be a rehearsal, she thought. Except there was no director around.

A hairy brute of a man called out as she approached the table. "Well, 'ere's a pretty 'un, eh, Clovis?"

Liv gave him an icy smile. "Ale all around, gentlemen." She ignored the hairy one and thumped the glasses down on the table, proud that she didn't spill a drop.

The one called Clovis, a dirty-looking man with a stained tunic, looked up at her through watery eyes. "Wherever be ye from, wench. I never 'eard such a tongue as yers."

"From near London," she answered, trying to mimic their accent and failing miserably. She was definitely among professional actors and couldn't compete.

"A London wench," another man remarked. "I wager she could show me a thing or two."

"Nothing you haven't seen before," Liv retorted tartly, and then watched, pleased when the men broke into laughter. She was holding her own in the role.

Weren't serving wenches supposed to be brash and bo-somy? So, what if she wasn't a perfect ten in the buxom department? No problem.

Satisfied with her performance, Liv turned to leave the table, and that's when the old geezer pinched her!

She whirled to confront him. Playing a role was one thing, capturing the spirit of the times, maybe even *faking* a pinch. But this was too much.

She put down her tray, ready to dress him down, but before she could deliver the lecture that was forming in her head, the door to the tavern was flung open. A man stepped across the threshold, silhouetted in a circle of candlelight and, at his appearance, the room grew stonily quiet.

He almost filled the doorway with his tall, broad frame. His black hair flowed to his shoulders, and his cape hung in soft folds from his shoulders.

Her rescuer!

He strode arrogantly across the still-silent room and chose a table in the back where he unfastened his cape and threw it dramatically over an empty chair. Paying no attention to anyone, he sat down at the candlelit ta-ble. For the first time, Liv saw his face in the light, and she felt her knees go weak.

"I don't believe it," she whispered to herself. The man in the tavern, the very same man who'd swept her onto his horse, was the Highwayman of her book!

For a long time, Liv stood and stared at him. This kind of thing didn't happen, certainly not to her, but something very weird was going on, and it was getting stranger by the minute.

She turned back toward the bar where Nora stood, like all the others, silent, watching. Liv rushed over to her just as conversation in the room resumed, more softly.

"Who is he?" she asked.

"That be Baron Northcliffe from the manor." Nora, too, kept her voice low as if she was afraid. "Oh, he's a bad 'un. Proud, he is, and some say downright dangerous. Ye'd best stay away from him, missy." With that admonition, Nora bustled off.

The man identified as Baron Northcliffe sat at the table, his legs extended. Liv remained at the bar, totally uninterested in continuing her role, but completely caught up in the aura of the man who had swept her up onto his horse and brought her here. She studied him intently.

The same high, proud forehead as the man in her book. The same straight nose and chiseled lips. A strong cleft chin. Black hair waving almost to his shoulders. Of course, the picture in the book was a portrait, an artist's rendition of the man, but sitting at the corner table was the one who could have posed for that portrait.

His shirt was white with full sleeves, and a white cravat was looped carelessly around his neck. His pants—Liv remembered they were called breeches—were black and skintight. So damned tight there could be no way he had a stitch on under them. She couldn't see the rest of his legs under the table, but she could use her imagination.

Watching him, a little quiver of anticipation grew inside her. Whether intentional or not, sensuality emanated from the so-called Baron Northcliffe like heat from a flame. He slouched insolently in his chair, lost in his own world and ignoring everyone around him.

But Liv wasn't ignoring him; in fact, she couldn't take her eyes off him. Not only did he look like the portrait in the book, his name was the same—Northcliffe. Obviously, the festival organizers had found a modern-day look-alike to impersonate the historical baron for the festival. What his connection was with New York State and the town of Chester, she couldn't imagine, but the resemblance was uncanny.

Liv sauntered over to his table. She'd thank him for the rescue, compliment him on the role he was playing—and find out his real name.

She couldn't get over how good-looking he was, as handsome as the man in *Rogues Across Time*. She tried to calm her nerves as she approached him, but her pulse was racing, and she was sure her cheeks were flushed with excitement.

She paused at his table, and he looked up at her with smoldering dark eyes. "Ah, yes, my riding companion." His lips curved in a roguish half smile. "If not a kiss, then perchance you could bring me a glass of ale?"

2

"ALE, it is—and my treat," Liv answered. "But first I want to thank you again for the rescue. I had no idea you were part of this, this—festival or whatever it is. And I sure didn't know I was going to be involved in it."

She leaned toward him and lowered her voice. "After tonight's little amusement is over, maybe you'll let me in on the secrets of your characterization." She wondered if there'd be a party when the festival ended. What was it called in the movie business, a wrap party? Well, this wasn't the movies, but it sure was make-believe. "My role, of course, was unexpected because . . ."

He looked at her with a mixture of confusion and disbelief, as if he didn't understand what she was talking about—or as if he disapproved of someone in her lowly station addressing him so casually in public. Had to be that, she decided. Playing his part perfectly. Maybe he wanted to win the award for best actor.

"I get the picture," she said. "No breaking character for a while." She managed a half curtsy. "I'll be right back with the ale, Sir—or Lord— What do you call a baron, anyway?"

He raised a sardonic eyebrow. "I expect these good folk have many names for me," he replied, nodding toward the other patrons. "Perhaps you should inquire of them."

"Great answer," Liv responded as she headed to the bar. "Witty and yet intriguing. And an ad-lib, at that."

"How'm I doing?" she asked Simon as he filled a mug with ale.

"Ye could move a bit faster and not be dawdlin' with the baron. Best leave him be."

She suppressed a smile. "Whatever you say, boss."

As she turned back toward the baron's table, she noticed his black eyes watching her questioningly. She couldn't stop looking at him, either. On top of his killer good looks, she couldn't get over the uncanny resemblance between this baron and the one in her book.

There had to be an explanation, and the only one she could come up with was a family connection. But after so many generations? She remembered pictures of her great-grandmother, thinking, *God help me if I look like her!*

She deposited his ale on the table with a flourish, not sure which of her many questions to ask him first. He took a long draft of ale and gazed at her over the rim of the tankard. Yes, he was damned good-looking.

"'Tis nice to have a pretty barmaid wait upon me. Sometimes the atmosphere at the Boot and Bottle is quite cold."

"I'll have to speak to the management," she quipped. "We wouldn't want you going to another tavern."

He threw back his head and laughed. "Not likely, as this is the only one. And I rather enjoy playing cat and mouse with the townsfolk."

"What a great script," she declared. "Have you thought about—"

Simon's voice thundered across the tavern. "Our customers are waitin' on their ale, girl. Are yer shoes nailed to the floor?"

Liv sighed. She'd never seen actors so dedicated to their roles. "I'll be back," she promised the baron in a stage whisper.

As she went from table to table, delivering mugs of ale, avoiding rapacious pinches on her behind, she caught snatches of gossip about the baron. Each man who played a villager was deep into his performance and had the background of the lead player figured out. That was really what you'd call researching a role, Liv decided.

She stopped to listen.

"The old baron, he were a terror before he died. Mad as they come, from drink they say," an elderly man confided to those at his table.

"Clear out of his mind," another agreed, "when he gambled away most of the family money and a fair share of the horses. Them was the finest racing stock in the land, horseflesh like none of ye ever see'd."

"I know that, I do," someone piped up. "Stratton colors was always flying in the winner's circle."

A man at the next table responded dryly. "Horses or no, the way things is goin', young Northcliffe won't get nowhere hisself. His day of reckoning will come."

"There's not proof agin him," another said stalwartly. "And to give the devil his due, the baron still drinks with us common folk."

A toothless, wizened man gave a cackle. "'Cause the fine lords and ladies won't entertain him, afeared as they are he might leave the party with their pretty baubles."

"Could be he's up to no good this very night," an elderly man muttered.

Liv got the evil eye from Nora and tore herself away from the table, carrying her tray of empty mugs. Her arms and shoulders were aching, and she decided it was time for the game to end. She moved among the tables, picking up empty mugs on her way to the bar and thinking about the conversations she'd just heard. As she reached a table near the door, she was almost run over by a young man who rushed into the tavern.

His fair hair was blown wildly about his face, and his eyes blazed with such intensity that Liv instinctively shrank back.

She rushed to the bar and plopped down her tray as his voice blared across the room.

"Northcliffe," he shouted. "I've come for ye."

As Liv watched, mesmerized, the angry young man, apparently very drunk, staggered toward the baron's table with his hands clenched into fists.

There was going to be a staged fight, Liv decided, fascinated. She'd rarely seen such realistic acting. "He's wonderful," she muttered as the burly actor confronted the man portraying Baron Northcliffe.

"Ye did it," he shouted. "Ye killed her!"

The room grew still as death, the rest of the audience as intent as Liv, watching the actor hurl himself across the room.

But the baron wasn't ready for a brawl. He surged from his chair and grabbed the man's arm. Then the scenario speedily unfolded, and the baron twisted back his attacker's arm with the ease of a man bending a twig. She expected to hear the crack of the young man's arm breaking; instead, there came an ear-piercing scream.

This was realism and more! The baron subdued his assailant and brought him to his knees before loosening his grasp. Then he spoke quietly. "You have no business talking to your better in such disrespectful terms. I should horsewhip you. But seeing you are the worse for drink, I will let you go." He called out imperiously to Simon. "Get this man out of the tavern and see that someone takes him home."

Liv was transfixed at the compelling drama of the situation. The room remained quiet as everyone watched the baron, his handsome, aristocratic face dark with anger, his eyes blazing. He dropped a few coins on the table and retrieved his cape. His eyes swept the room in a fierce look.

When his gaze reached Liv, she held her breath. His eyes were hypnotic, smoldering, full of fire and mystery. Liv felt her knees go weak as their gazes locked. A shadow of a smile flickered momentarily on his lips. His words were for her and her alone.

"I shall have that kiss yet, lass. I always get what I want." He swung the cape over his shoulders, turned and stalked out the door. Liv couldn't resist applauding. His performance had been brilliant.

"Bravo!" she shouted, expecting the other spectators to join in her cheers.

Instead, Nora grabbed her hands. "What is this foolishness, wench, acting like ye was at a theater?"

Liv gave a sigh of exasperation. "Oh, come off it, Nora. I'm in on the joke. You're having a festival here, and this is a reenactment of some historical event. Baron Northcliffe . . . the murder of some woman . . ."

The young man, who was being hauled up by a friend, responded angrily. "He done it! He killed my Betsy just like he killed them other maidens."

Simon moved quickly. "John Darcy, ye need to get out of here and on yer way home. Someone will go along with ye, for safety's sake."

Darcy pulled away from Simon's grasp. "The man's a thief, he is, and a murderer. And he gets away with it, so high and mighty—"

"Get him out," Simon ordered, and it was done, by two burly yeomen, leaving the mood in the tavern somber.

"What's the next plot twist?" Liv asked Nora. "I know the real baron was hanged, but I can't remember why. Was it for killing a village woman?"

"Hanged?" Nora looked at her askance.

"According to my book, he *was* hanged. Of course, this version may be different." She paused and thought about that. "I certainly would have changed the facts if I were producing the reenactment because from his picture, the baron is anything but a murderer." She turned to Nora. "I don't know if you've seen it, but I'm sure the director has. That actor looks exactly like him."

"Ye're talking nonsense, girl."

"Then talk *plain* sense, and tell me what really is going on."

"I'll tell ye then, just so ye'll get on with the work. Ye've done little enough tonight."

Liv bit back sharp words about being drafted into waitressing with hardly a thank-you. She kept quiet because she wanted to hear the story.

"Ever since the young baron come back to North-cliffe Manor, he's been tearin' 'cross the countryside on that black horse like the devil hisself. There's somethin' afoot, 'specially with the Highwayman also a-ridin'—"

"The Highwayman! What a romantic character!" Liv exclaimed. "I love it."

Nora wrinkled her nose. "Ye have the strangest way of thinking, girl. I tell ye that the Highwayman's ridin' for sure, but he don't bother us plain folks. He robs the nobles, them leaving parties and balls and sich."

"Like Robin Hood," Liv said, delighted. This was getting better and better. "Does he rob from the rich and give to the poor?"

"Hmmph! If he does, this poor woman ain't seen a farthing of his riches," Nora answered tartly. "Now then, wench," she said, pointing to a crowded table, "that bunch's getting low on ale—"

"First, tell me, please, about this murder accusation. Who does John Darcy think the baron killed?"

Nora sighed grandly and crossed her arms over her ample bosom. "I can see ye won't get any work done until it's all told. And mayhaps ye should know for safety's sake. Betsy and John was to be married in a fortnight, but she were killed. Found up in the hills, strangled. And she weren't the only one. Two more maidens has been found dead—and all since the young baron come back to town."

"Circumstantial evidence," Liv said airily. "But it makes a good tale. Can ye—I mean *you*—tell me the name of the man who played Baron Northcliffe. I'd like to compliment him on his acting ability—"

"Ye think he's acting?" Nora burst into laughter. "There you go with that theater talk again. If that don't beat all—"

"Please, Nora, if that's your real name. It's time to cut to the chase. I'm not participating any longer. I'm going to my room to take a bath and call a garage about my rental car. I've been sidetracked long enough. Besides, I've paid my dues for the town's little historical pageant."

Liv handed her apron to Nora. Then she noticed the woman's face, bright red with anger.

"Ye must be daft, wench, talking to me like that. Ye won't leave here until I say. My brother told me ye were a little slow, but looks to me like ye're downright brainless."

Furious, Liv calmed herself long enough to reply, "I'm going upstairs right now and no one, I mean no one, can stop me." Holding her head high, she swept out of the tavern.

SHE IGNORED Nora's angry cries as she rushed into the lobby. It was illuminated by a smoky lantern, and in the dim light she noticed that the check-in desk had gone— disappeared, and along with it the charming little woman who acted as the inn's concierge. Gone, too, were the telephone, the huge arrangement of fresh flowers and the grouping of antique chairs that had given the inn its charm.

"These people are serious," Liv muttered, "redecorating the whole damn place."

She looked for the light switch at the bottom of the stairs, and when she couldn't find it, she grabbed a lantern from the table and took the steps two at a time, eager to escape into the sanctity—and sanity—of her room. When she opened her door, the second one on the right, she felt her heart jump in her throat.

It wasn't her room! She stepped back into the hall and looked for the number but couldn't find it. Yet this had been her room when she checked in this morning.

She held up the lantern, trying to control her mounting hysteria. This was no illusion. Everything was different. There were no flowered chintz curtains at the window, no lamps or telephone. And instead of the low double bed with its fluffy comforter, there was a lumpy-looking four-poster.

She crossed the room, opened the wardrobe and looked inside. Her clothes, suitcase, cosmetics kit, even her briefcase, were gone. She'd been robbed!

She sank onto the lumpy bed and stared at the clothes hanging in place of hers, men's clothes from another century—knee breeches, frock coat, frilled shirt. Was she losing her mind?

A shiver crawled up her spine. This had to be the worst day of her life, her car in a ditch, her clothes stolen—not to mention being caught in the middle of a bizarre "happening" of some sort.

Get it together, she advised herself. It had been obvious from the beginning that the town was putting on a reenactment. Now, for some reason, the actors had taken over rooms in the inn which clearly had been redecorated.

All right. Then where were her clothes? Moved to another room, of course!

She bounded up, out the door and raced down the hall, moving from room to room, knocking, throwing open doors, looking inside. All of them were dark, empty, furnished from another era. None of them held her clothes.

Still grasping the lantern, Liv tore back down the stairs and burst into the tavern. Most of the patrons had left, and only a few huddled in a corner playing cards. Simon looked up from the bar. "Here she be, Nora."

"Maybe ye should take the strap to her," his wife responded.

"Stop this nonsense!" Liv shouted. "I want some answers, and I want them now. Who are you? What's going on? Where are my clothes? Where am *I*? When will this damned charade end?"

Nora ignored the questions. "Stop wailin' like a banshee, wench. We've told ye, we're Nora and Simon Trueblood and this be our inn." A satisfied smile spread across her round face. "The Boot and Bottle. And that's where ye's at."

"Now, girl, it's time for ye to be tellin' us somethin'," Simon said.

His wife piped up. "Just who is ye, anyway? Not the serving wench me brother sent, that's a fact."

"You're right," Liv agreed. "I'm not a serving *wench*. I'm Olivia Johnson, and I checked in this morning because my grandparents' farm is nearby, just a few miles from the town of Chester, and I—"

"Chester?" Simon interrupted. "'Tis no sich town hereabouts."

"Of course there is. *This* is the town of Chester in New York State," Liv insisted. "Columbia County. The Hudson River Valley."

"Poor child is daft as a daisy," Simon said to his wife as he looked at Liv pityingly. "This here is Yorkshire, England, more particularly, the town of Haroldsgate."

"Please don't joke with me anymore. I really can't take it," Liv moaned. "Enough is enough."

"Then stop trying to pull the wool over our eyes," Nora commanded. "This here is Haroldsgate, all right, and if ye don't believe it, look out the door. 'Tis Haroldsgate outside, as well." She gave Liv a push. "Go see."

"All right, I will." She opened the door and looked into the night.

Darkness. Everywhere. No light in the whole town. Nothing but the night and the whine of the wind in the trees. Liv didn't know what was happening, but if this was a joke, it was a huge one that involved the whole town. It included turning off all the electricity and changing, even moving, some of the buildings.

She turned away, and Simon closed the door behind her as Liv walked slowly back toward the bar, her head spinning. What if this wasn't a joke or a trick? What if . . . Her mind refused to accept the thought. It was impossible; she couldn't be in England!

Liv tried to speak, but her throat was dry, and a band of fear had tightened around her chest. She felt her body weave back and forth, and she put her hands on her temples to stop the movement.

"Dear Lord, the girl's going to swoon on us," Nora cried, her irritation turned to concern.

"She's pale as if she'd seen a ghost," Simon intoned.

"I have," Liv croaked. "You!" She sank into a chair, her knees like jelly. Either she was crazy or everyone around her was. Neither possibility was very encouraging. Tears welled in her eyes as she looked up at the couple, who were now standing close together, watching her anxiously.

"Please," she beseeched, "help me. Tell me why this is happening. And if it's a joke, call it off. I'll be happy to declare you the winner."

Nora looked at her and then at Simon. "If this don't beat all. We ask for a wench to help out, and we git a sickly, puny thing who's daft, to boot. We should be sending her back."

"Not tonight," Simon said.

"Then what d'ye suggest we do with her?"

"Let her sleep in the attic. She's too befuddled to help with the washing up."

"That's a fact," Nora admitted. "Then git on upstairs, girl."

"To the attic? You don't understand! I booked a room here, a lovely room—a little overdecorated, but still—" Liv stopped midsentence. The couple was clearly mystified. Liv got shakily to her feet. "All right. I'll go to bed—in the attic. I'm so tired, I could probably sleep anywhere." She picked up the lantern.

"And when I wake up, I'll be home because this is a dream. That's the only explanation. It's just a bad dream."

Nora rolled her eyes. "Such gibberish, I've never heard." She reached over and took the lantern from Liv's hand. "I'll keep that down here. We can't be wasting oil, and the candle'll be good enough for ye."

Liv accepted the candle and clutched it in her trembling hand. "There's one more thing. You say I'm in England, in a town called Haroldsgate." She wet her dry lips with her tongue. "So tell me, what year is it?"

Nora shook her head. "She don't even know the date."

"Why, it be the month of June in the year of our Lord 1796," Simon said. "And King George the Third sits on the throne of England."

IN THE DANK ATTIC, Liv lay curled in a little ball on a narrow cot. Her candle had burned down to a stub and gone out, leaving the tiny room in complete darkness. She had never felt so alone in her life or prayed so hard for sleep to come.

But she remained wide-awake, her nerves tingling, her pulse racing as her mind played over the events of the evening. She tried to put them together into a complete picture, but the pieces simply didn't fit.

First, there was the picture of Baron Northcliffe in *Rogues Across Time*, then the man on horseback, the inn where she had registered only hours before—except it was different—and the town festival, the reenactment, if that's what it was. Nothing fit! She felt like screaming.

Instead, she pulled the blanket more tightly around her, with one thought wedged in her mind: in real life after the show was over, the actors went home, turned on the lights, brewed a pot of coffee and watched TV. None of that seemed to be happening here.

"A joke of some kind? A trick? But why? Why?" she murmured into her lumpy pillow. Had Peggy hatched this bizarre plot to drive Liv crazy and steal the farm? Maybe the land was worth millions, and everyone in town was part of the scheme.

Liv felt the tears rising in her eyes again. There was no conspiracy, and she knew it. That was the stuff of novels, not real life. There was only one logical explanation, the one she'd come to downstairs with Simon and Nora: she was asleep and dreaming. Or in a coma, hallucinating. Soon she'd wake up, at home. Or in the inn—the real inn, the one she'd checked into. Or in a hospital where a kindly doctor would explain how she'd been unconscious for a few hours.

All she had to do was fall asleep, without benefit of aspirin for her aching head. When she woke up, there'd be no more Haroldsgate or Boot and Bottle, no more dark, handsome baron on his fierce black stallion.

"Damn him," she cried. "He's the cause of it all. He's the one who's making me think I'm in the eighteenth century. But I'm not! This isn't 1796, and I'm not in England. I'm not, I'm not, I'm not . . ."

She repeated the words like a litany until she finally fell into a restless sleep.

LIV TOOK a half step into the street, squinting in the early-morning light. Out of the corner of her eye, she caught a glimpse of a huge, shadowy shape hurtling down on her. She heard the frightening sounds of snorting horses, the crack of a leather whip and a voice that boomed at her.

"Out of the road, wench!"

Liv jumped back into the safety of a doorway to avoid being run down. Two horses pulling a carriage veered around the corner, the driver high on his perch, a long whip in his gloved hand. The carriage creaked and groaned as it passed within inches of her. She caught a glimpse of someone inside, a man, whose eyes met hers, coldly, before he reached up and closed the curtain. Then the carriage was gone, roaring down the road.

Leaning back against the building in an attempt to keep her legs from buckling, Liv realized that she'd experienced a near accident that was too real to deny. This wasn't make-believe, and it wasn't a dream.

When she'd awoken, she'd found herself in the same tiny attic room where she'd fallen asleep the night before. She'd slipped out of the tavern, careful to avoid Simon and Nora, holding on to the hope that once she got outside into the sunlight, everything would be all right. She'd be awake and back in the twentieth century.

Well, she was awake, all right. Her near miss with the carriage proved that. It also proved this wasn't the twentieth century. She looked down the street that ran through the little village. More proof, if she needed it. Next to the Boot and Bottle was a blacksmith shop, and beyond that, an apothecary. Across the street, a little church and graveyard. And if she wanted to really drive herself bananas, Liv needed only to cross that street and read the dates on the tombstones. She knew there wouldn't be a single one later than 1796.

So much for the dead. The living were everywhere. Along the streets walked women in long dresses and bonnets, men in breeches and frock coats. There were more horses and carriages, moving slower than the one that almost ran her down, children playing and dogs barking. An idyllic English-village scene.

And she was in the middle of it.

She wanted to yell until help came, but she knew that her only salvation lay within herself. Something strange had happened to her, something that went beyond what she knew of time and space. For a while she had to suspend disbelief and accept the fact that she,

Olivia Johnson, jewelry designer from New York City, was in Haroldsgate, England, in the year 1796.

It was impossible; yet it was real. She might as well accept it. What choice did she have? "All right," she said aloud, "let the game begin."

She'd made a quick decision and decided to act on it, approaching a portly man walking along the street. His demeanor was prosperous and genteel, his face big and open above his high collar and double-breasted blue coat.

"Excuse me, sir. I wonder if you'd be good enough to tell me where Baron Northcliffe lives? I need to..." Her voice trailed off. What she needed to do was almost unexplainable.

"Northcliffe? You want the manor house, a good five miles outside of town."

His answer given, he turned as if to walk away, and Liv realized that he was a gentleman and she looked like a mere serving wench. He was probably offended that she'd even approached him. She dropped an awkward curtsy and called out.

"Pardon me, sir, for taking your time, but is there a shortcut across the fields?"

He pointed. "Go half a mile or so and then turn east. There will be a stile over a fence. You will cross a field and ford a stream, but the walk will be shorter for you."

"Thank you, sir, thank you kindly." Liv dipped again into her curtsy.

As she set off along the rutted road, she felt the man's eyes on her. She probably seemed as foreign to him as this whole damned place did to her, Liv thought as she avoided a rumbling cart pulled by a shaggy pony. She considered hitching a ride on the back, but figured she'd be noticed and booted off. Not being dressed like a lady was a real problem when a person landed in another century, Liv decided wryly.

She headed east, following the morning sun, determined to find the notorious baron. That's the decision she'd made, for lack of any other possibility. Baron Northcliffe was her only connection with Haroldsgate or the year 1796. She'd seen his picture in the book, and had been thinking about him as she drove along the foggy road yesterday. Then, after the crash, she'd ended up in his world.

The book and the baron were eerily tied together, and in some inexplicable way, she'd become trapped in their cosmic connection.

This was the most frightening thing that had ever happened to her, but she had two choices. To give in to her fear and withdraw into a whimpering, cringing ball of insanity. Or to play out the role she'd been given, Liv Johnson, serving wench of Haroldsgate. But she couldn't play it out at the inn. Simon and Nora had already decided to send her back where she came from. And she had the suspicion that she wouldn't be going back to New York in 1996 but some obscure English village far from here—in the year 1796.

She'd already been alone with the baron, on a dark foggy night, and no harm had come to her. He certainly hadn't attempted to cut her throat! As for his reputation as a highwayman, that didn't scare her half as much as her present situation.

So the baron was going to get a caller.

Half an hour later, Liv caught a glimpse of the stile and turned off the road toward the field. She paused at the top of the steps that spanned the split-rail fence and looked around at the bucolic scene spread out in the distance. Summer was everywhere. Fields were bright green, and fleecy clouds dotted the blue sky. In the distance was a small farmhouse with a thatched roof, surrounded by a garden. A cow grazed near the house, and smoke rose lazily from a chimney. The scene was idyllic.

She sank onto the steps, reached in her pocket and pulled out a wedge of game pie she'd stolen from the empty tavern kitchen. She chewed it thoughtfully, unable to avoid the irony of the situation. All her life she'd strived to be someone special, successful and respected. And now in some bizarre twist of fate, she'd ended up as a damn serving woman! Well, she'd had little choice. She'd just have to play the role well; it wasn't in her nature to do otherwise.

The pie had given her enough energy to go on, and she strode purposefully across the field, praying she was doing the right thing.

NORTHCLIFFE MANOR hovered above Liv—gray stone, three stories high with a great dome rising from the roof and a huge front porch supported by pillars. It looked like a Roman temple, and it depressed her terribly. Obviously, the house had been very beautiful and stately at one time, probably a real showplace. Now it looked neglected and sinister.

Maybe her attic room at the inn wasn't so bad, after all, Liv thought. But its owners weren't about to pay attention to what they called her "daft ravings." Besides, the baron had gotten her into this mess; the baron was going to get her out of it, she told herself, walking resolutely toward the house.

She climbed the stone steps to the porch, remembering that it was properly called a portico. That was the extent of her knowledge of architecture, but it wasn't going to do her any good this morning, anyway. What she needed now was a little courage. She reached in her pocket and curled her fingers around the can of pepper spray. If the baron turned out to be the menace to society Nora indicated, at least she could defend herself.

With that, she took a deep breath and knocked on the huge front door. The sound echoed hollowly. She tried again, and when there was no response, she turned the heavy handle. The door opened, and Liv stepped into the manor house.

The marble entry hall soared high to a domed ceiling. There were deep niches in the wall, some of them supporting statues, others strangely empty. She could barely make out a carved staircase which curved upward and seemed to disappear. The whole effect was cold and forbidding.

Well, she'd gotten this far. There was no turning back now. "Hello," she called out. "Anybody home?"

Getting no response, she walked silently, nervously, down the dim hall past closed doors. Family portraits in gilt frames lined the walls, unsmiling men staring down at her.

One of them stopped her in her tracks. She looked up in disbelief. It was the face from her book!

The original portrait of the baron of Northcliffe held her for a long moment, his dark eyes mesmerizing. Finally, with an audible moan, she tore her gaze away. What the hell was going on?

Taking a deep breath, she moved toward a half-open door and stealthily peered inside. There he was. The man in the portrait. Baron Northcliffe. Her heart began to beat faster. He was as handsome as she remembered, more handsome than in the portrait on the wall—and in the book that had brought her here.

He was dressed as before, in a white shirt of fine cotton material, tight black breeches and boots, and his hair was carelessly combed back from his face.

He was seated at a massive curved mahogany desk, bent over a ledger. He didn't look at all happy.

Liv cleared her throat timorously.

"Migod, you gave me a start!" He looked up from his work. "The tavern serving girl! Who let you in?"

"No one. The door was open—"

"And you decided to let *yourself* in." He got up from the chair and leaned over, his hands on the desktop. "Were you not warned about me in the tavern?" He lifted a sardonic eyebrow. "After all, I do have a reputation."

Liv met his eyes evenly. "I don't believe any of the gossip I've heard about the dangerous Baron Northcliffe."

"Then you are a foolish wench. Unless," he added softly, "you have a liking for danger."

Liv retreated a step, but her voice was strong. "If you'd wanted to hurt me, you could have done so in the fog last eventide with no one the wiser." She flashed a smile. "Why, I'm beginning to get into the eighteenth-century vernacular!"

The baron shook his head. Her words were gibberish, but the wench herself was robust and full of life. This could be very interesting, he thought as he heard her out.

"But you didn't harm me. Instead, you rescued me, and I'm not afraid." She lifted her chin challengingly.

"Then why are you here?"

"It's very difficult to explain, but I believe you're the only person who can help figure out what's happened to me. The way you appeared out of the fog could be a sign that you're the key to the mystery. You see . . ."

As she talked, he studied her more closely. She chattered about "cars" and "garages" and "magic carpets," words totally meaningless. The town she spoke of, Chester, was not in these parts, to his knowledge. And she had an accent that was not English, Irish or Scots. He'd certainly heard nothing like it on the continent. However outlandish her speech, she seemed totally involved in her story.

He was more interested in the woman herself. He let his eyes wander up and down her form. She was taller than any woman he knew, but nicely rounded, with firm breasts and a slender waist that flowed into slim hips.

He especially liked her hair. Wind-tossed, shades of honey, wheat and bronze, all blended together into a deep tawny mass that fell to her shoulders. She had a seductive manner of pushing it away from her face as she talked.

Her eyes were the color of summer bluebells, and her lashes and brows were a darker shade of honey, contrasting with the peachy color of her complexion. He let his eyes dwell on her mouth. A full, sensuous mouth, made for kisses, above a strong round chin.

A satisfied smile curved his lips. Fate, for a change, had been kind to him, delivering such a delicious surprise, so early in the morning. Last night's unfortunate events had cut his evening in the tavern short. But here she was, in his library, obviously available ... and willing.

"And so you'll understand," she said, finishing her long and convoluted story, "that I had to come and see you."

The baron moved from behind his desk, closer to the woman. He could see a faint pulse beating in her throat. From nervousness or excitement? He felt his own heart pound a little faster from the unexpected visit—and the possibilities it presented. He was drawn to her, aroused by her closeness. For an hour or so, she might lighten the burdens he bore.

He moved around the desk, close to her, noticing that she didn't draw back. He touched the soft tangles of her hair. Her eyes widened, and that's when she moved away, or tried to. He took hold of her arms and pulled her close, feeling her struggle against him, enjoying the movement of her breasts and hips.

"You don't understand," she cried. "I'm not—"

He held her more tightly and lowered his mouth toward hers. "No more talking. There is only one reason why a serving wench would visit a nobleman, entering through the front door and coming into his private library. We both know what that reason is."

She opened her mouth in protest, but before she could speak, he covered it hungrily with his own.

3

LIV'S SURPRISE changed suddenly to pleasure as his mouth pressed against hers, leaving her breathless and shaky. Then he insinuated his tongue between her lips, and she felt a knot of forbidden desire tighten deep inside. Her breasts were pushed against his broad chest, and the friction caused by the movement of his body was intoxicating. So was the warmth of his hands cupping her bottom and pressing her thighs more tightly against his.

The thrill she felt was wild and wicked and couldn't be denied. But it was also bizarre, by far the strangest predicament in her twenty-four hours of craziness. How could it be happening—a twentieth-century woman kissing an eighteenth-century man—and enjoying it! And obviously he was enjoying it, too.

When he pulled her even closer and deepened the kiss, Liv tried to get her thoughts in order. Another few minutes—or even few seconds—and she would be in big trouble.

It was time to stop this nonsense. She pushed against his chest, intensely aware of the coiled strength of his muscles, but determined to escape from his powerful arms.

That was easier said than done. She pushed again, harder, and squirmed against him, but he held fast. He wasn't going to let her go.

The hell he wasn't! She bit down on his bottom lip.

Letting out a curse that dated back to Chaucer, he pushed her away and put his hand to his mouth. He looked down, first at the red stain on his fingertips, and then at her. "Damn you, wench! You've drawn blood."

Liv didn't like the look that flashed in his dark eyes just as it had the night before in the tavern. Instinctively, she moved a little farther from him, looking around for a way out.

"I should turn you across my knee."

That did it. She stopped, hands on her hips, and regarded him with eyes blazing. "You wouldn't dare."

"Dare? This is my house, woman!" he roared. "I do what I please."

He moved toward her, and Liv ran for cover—behind his big mahogany desk. "And if *you* please me—"

She wasn't fooling herself into thinking that the desk would protect her. All he had to do was reach out with his big hands, his strong arms, and drag her from her sanctuary.

Then she saw the ivory-handled letter opener on the desktop. It was probably ten inches long, and as sharp as a dagger. She grabbed the weapon and held it with both hands, poised to defend herself.

"Oh, no, Buster," she threatened. "Don't you try anything with me. I didn't come here to be groped."

At that, his expression changed, and he threw back his head, laughing.

"What in the world—" His reaction startled her.

"Groped," he said, laughing again.

At first, Liv thought maybe he didn't understand the word. With practically no knowledge of late eighteenth-century English, she had no idea what words were familiar to him. But his next comment told her that he knew exactly what she was talking about.

"My attentions have never been described as such. Groped! No woman has ever said this to me. Certainly not a wench like yourself, who invited my attentions, if I recall correctly."

"I did not! How dare you!"

He balanced on the balls of his feet like a great cat, his eyes narrowed, a slight smile teasing his chiseled lips.

She was incensed by the smile and had an overwhelming desire to wipe it off his smug, aristocratic face. She swung the letter opener in an arc in front of her. "I'm warning you, I can be lethal."

Without dropping his gaze, he brought his arm to his mouth, blotting the blood she'd drawn onto the white fabric. "Indeed," he said. As he looked straight into her eyes, Liv noticed he was unflinching, no longer smiling and just a little intimidating.

And he made her feel damned foolish. To regain authority, she brandished the letter opener again. But it was too late. He'd obviously seen the hesitation in her eyes, and moved suddenly, without warning, just as he had in the tavern. His hand shot out and grabbed her wrist.

She tried to twist away, but that only made him intensify his grip. The letter opener clattered harmlessly to the floor. With easy strength, he pulled her around the desk and close to him.

She winced as his fingers dug into her wrist, but she remained stoic, returning his dark gaze unflinchingly.

He pushed her backward and let go of her, and she fell into a strategically placed wing chair.

"Now that I am convinced you did not come here for my kisses, tell me," he ordered in a serious voice, "who are you and what do you want?"

Liv sat up straight in the chair, her shoulders back and head high, meeting his eyes directly although her heart was pounding. "I told you, and you paid no attention."

He hooked his boot around the leg of a stool, pulled it toward him and sat down. On her level now, he wasn't any less intimidating. "Tell me again," he said, leaning toward her.

"Well, I—"

"You rode a magic carpet, I believe."

"No . . . that's the name of the bookstore where I—"

"A carriage, then."

"Please stop answering your own questions!" When he was silent for a couple of seconds, she quickly plunged in. "It wasn't a magic carpet or a carriage. I got here in my car. My automobile."

He remained silent, not reacting to the word which, Liv realized, he didn't understand.

"It's like a carriage, but there are no horses," she explained. Then she remembered the term. "A horseless carriage."

"Of course," he responded sarcastically.

He got up and moved to the desk with a look that told her she wasn't going anywhere, so she might as well keep trying to explain until she convinced him—if that were even possible.

"I know it sounds odd to you, your, uh, lordship . . ." She stopped midsentence, but he didn't offer to help her out with his title. "The thing that's probably even harder for you to understand is that I don't belong here in your house. Or in your century. As I've tried to tell you, I'm from the twentieth century. The year 1996, exactly two hundred years from now, as a matter of fact. I was driving in my car—well, my horseless carriage—and I ran off the road. When I woke up, I was here. In England. Which is doubly odd because I started out in New York." She stopped and sighed. "That's in the United States—in America."

"Ah, yes, America. The colonies."

"They *were* the colonies. But your King George the Third lost them during the Revolutionary War, just twenty years ago, in fact."

"So I have heard," he replied with a rueful twist to his words. He leaned back against his massive desk, his arms crossed, and regarded her intently.

"I don't understand anything that happened to me," she said. "And here's the really odd thing. I had a book in the car, a book I'd bought only a few minutes before I went into the ditch. I know this is going to sound crazy, but the book had your picture in it."

His only reaction was a narrowing of his black eyes.

"So that's why I recognized you. And it did seem, well, almost cosmically arranged—preordained, you might say, that you were the one to come upon me in the fog. To rescue me." She paused for a moment, knowing how bizarre her story must sound to him.

"I don't believe in time travel or the supernatural or any of that kind of thing," she went on. "Not at all. But somehow it happened to me. I started out on a foggy summer afternoon in New York and ended up two hundred years earlier in the English countryside. It makes me crazy, let me tell you, and I need help. Desperately. I'm sure you can understand."

He let out his breath slowly. Dear God, he thought, she was an appealing wench, and she was extremely clever. She'd gotten into his house, found him alone and managed to captivate him with her farfetched story.

"You have not told me your name, have you?"

"I will if you will," she said.

He smiled. "Fair enough. I am Baron Northcliffe."

"But you must have a first name."

"Of course. My given name is Gabriel, the family name Stratton."

"Do I call you sir?" she asked.

"You may."

"Sir Stratton."

He laughed. "No, Sir Gabriel."

"Not Lord Gabriel."

"Your lordship is the term of address. But it is Sir Gabriel. Or, if you wish, Baron Northcliffe."

"If I wish," she repeated, thinking to herself that she wasn't about to call him any of those names. She had another idea. "What about Gabe?"

"Gabe?" he repeated with a frown.

"It's a nickname. A diminutive," she coaxed.

"I see. From Gabriel."

"Sir Gabe!" she said, noting a glint in his eye.

He smiled slightly. "Of course, if you wish. Now tell me your name."

"Olivia Johnson, but most people call me Liv."

"A nickname," he replied, his smile mocking her now. "But I prefer to call you Olivia. From Shakespeare."

"Twelfth Night," she supplied.

He nodded slowly. "An actress from the London stage would know that. Perhaps one hired to play a role—"

"No," she interrupted. "I'm not an actress, and I wasn't hired to come here, although I can understand that would be a logical explanation. In fact, that was my first thought, too, that I'd been tricked into joining some kind of play at the tavern."

He was listening to her carefully now.

"That's why I applauded what I thought was your performance as Baron Northcliffe." She sank back in the chair. "But now I understand. It's neither a play nor a dream. It's real. Our kiss was real, wasn't it?"

He touched his lip again and smiled sardonically. "Very real, which makes your story of being transported in time even more difficult for me to believe. This is the Age of Enlightenment. A time of science and reason. In spite of your different way of speaking and your unusual expressions, I am sure there is a logical explanation. I do not believe in spirits or fairies or manifestations of the future."

She pushed her thick honey-colored hair back from her face. "Then tell me, what is your theory, Sir Gabe?"

She was a saucy wench, he thought, fearless, brazen and quick of wit. Sir Gabe, indeed! And he was letting her tease him. He'd certainly never given a woman, even one of his own class, that privilege.

"If not an actress, perhaps you have escaped from a lunatic asylum," he offered. "A devil of a situation, wouldn't you say?"

As he waited for her response, he kept another possibility to himself, the one uppermost in his mind. *Spy*. She need not have been a professional actress to get hired to spy on him by his enemies in the parish. But which of the scoundrels would it have been? Livingstone, Cardiff or Fremont, the high sheriff?

While he pondered that thought, she continued, "I know my story sounds crazy to you. It does to me, too. But I'm not insane, and I can prove everything happened just as I said. If you'll just help me find the car—and the book—then you'll see that everything I say is true. My car is there, in a ditch on the side of the road. But I can't find it alone. I need your help."

As she looked beseechingly at him, he tried to steel his emotions against her. A tantalizing woman such as this one could be a potent danger, and he had very nearly stepped into her web. But now, he knew the truth. He would play her game, all the while watching her like a hawk.

Liv tried to read the expression on his face. Skepticism, yes, but interest, also—and suspicion. Well, why wouldn't he be suspicious? Her story was unbelievable. She'd be lucky if he didn't cart her off to Bedlam.

"I think it best—" Gabriel broke off in midsentence when a man appeared at the library door. He had red hair and was shorter than the baron, and stockier, dressed in brown pants and a rumpled white shirt.

"Is it important, Michael?" Gabriel asked impatiently.

"It's about the chestnut stallion, your lordship."

"What about him?"

"Favoring that back leg again. Thought you should have a look before I apply the poultice."

With that, the baron turned on his heel, brushed past her and left the room, followed closely by Michael.

She was wondering what to do, when he returned and stopped in the doorway.

"Come along, if you care to."

She scurried after the two men, along the hall to the front portico and down the steps. There, in the circular driveway, was a huge horse, just as big and beautiful as the baron's black stallion, but this one's coat gleamed a rich brown. Holding the animal, or doing his best to, was a young boy, barely as high as the horse's shoulder.

"He's giving the groom a fit, sir."

"In some pain, no doubt," Gabe said as he strode over and put a firm hand on the halter.

As Liv watched, the animal seemed to calm down.

"Hold him steady, boy." Gabe moved around the horse slowly, talking softly, caressed the animal's flank and picked up the back foot. He rested it quickly and expertly between his knees and examined the hoof carefully.

There seemed to be a quiet communion between man and beast that was fascinating—and familiar—to watch. The gentle way he handled the stallion reminded Liv of her grandfather's way with his horses. The memory was comforting and made her feel less alone.

Then he released the hoof and stepped back. The horse reared up, pawing the air with his front feet, practically lifting the boy off the ground.

"Still has plenty of spirit," Gabe said casually to Michael as the poor groom held on for dear life.

"Spirit he has, sir, but he's not improving," Michael said, shaking his head.

"You are right about that, I'm sorry to say." Gabe and Michael walked back up the steps, past Liv, as the boy headed toward the stables, half dragging, half being dragged by the horse.

Liv figured her only choice was to follow the two men.

"I reckon it won't be long before we have to put him out to pasture, milord."

"Yes, I know," Gabe said sadly.

"But he can still go to stud. And there's a mare just perfect for breeding with him."

"Oh, and what mare is that?" They reached the library and went inside. Liv slipped into the room after them and sat down.

"Why, the very one at the auction in Newmarket. The Arabian."

"Oh, yes." Gabe paused, thoughtfully, and then looked over at Liv, as if seeing her for the first time since she followed them outside. "By the way, Michael, this is Mistress Olivia."

Olivia. Hearing her name on his lips gave her a little thrill. The way he said it made it sound as smooth and rich as Devon cream.

"She is visiting us from—" he arched a dark eyebrow "—far away. She is temporarily stranded and in need of help." His mouth twitched with what seemed to be the beginning of a smile. Liv had seen that half smile before and knew the irony in it.

"I'll be glad to take her to the kitchen and turn her over to Cook, if you'd like, sir," Michael offered.

The baron shook his head slowly. "No, I do not think so. Instead, I shall attempt to help her myself. Olivia, this is my steward, Michael McQuire, the finest judge of horseflesh in England."

She could see the faint blush that stained Michael's fair complexion at the compliment. She got to her feet and executed a half curtsy, not really sure if a serving wench should curtsy to an estate steward, but assuming that in her current incarnation she was on the lowest rung of society.

"Now, about the Arabian mare, Michael." Again, he dismissed Liv in favor of a discussion of horseflesh. Refusing to get insulted about the possible comparison, she made a face at Gabriel—behind his back—and moved to the bookcases, but not out of earshot of their conversation.

"She's a beauty, your lordship, Morning Star by name. Direct in line from the Godolphin Arabian."

"So they say?"

"'Tis true, milord. She's by Dark Knight out of Early Dawn. And if we could breed her to the chestnut stallion, there's not a horse in England could outrun the foal when it comes of racing age."

"Quite possibly," the baron answered. Liv glanced up from a first edition of Samuel Johnson's dictionary and saw that the baron was regarding his steward seriously.

"The chestnut's getting no younger nor healthier," Michael said.

"You are right, Michael. The black stallion has got years ahead of him, but we do not have as much time with the chestnut. Now, this mare, has she papers from the Arabian?"

"'Deed so, milord."

"Then it should be a good match."

"'Deed so," Michael repeated.

"We need only one more foal to win wearing the Stratton colors, and ours will once again be the finest racing family in this part of England. It will happen. That much I swear."

At the force of his words, Liv looked up and saw that his hand was clenched into a fist. For some reason, a little shiver ran along her spine. Her grandfather had held such hopes. But they were only dreams, really. Gabriel looked serious, and quite possibly obsessed.

Michael shuffled his feet uneasily. "Just a small problem, sir. Our accounts . . . Can we afford a mare such as Morning Star?"

"Not to worry, I will take care of that," Gabe said easily. "Let the referee know that the Stratton colors will be among the most prominent at the auction."

Liv slipped the leather-bound book back on the shelf. Michael didn't ask how the baron was going to obtain the money to buy the mare. That wasn't the steward's problem—or his business—but she had some ideas. He could sell the valuable books or the paintings that lined the walls. She was sure she recognized a Hogarth and possibly even a Reynolds. And then there were the family portraits, including the baron's. The artwork must be worth a fortune. As well, she'd noticed a collection of Wedgwood china in a glass-fronted cabinet. What in the world would that be worth? Then she realized she was thinking in 1996 terms. In 1796, the value might not even have been established.

It didn't matter, Liv decided. The baron had another way of getting the money, and she knew just what it was. Robbery. Playing the role of the Highwayman.

Michael stood quietly, nodding as Gabriel continued his instructions regarding the horse auction. But his forehead was creased in a frown of worry. "As you say, sir," he mouthed almost by rote.

"You attend to the bloodlines, and I will handle the rest."

With a nod and a bow, the still-concerned-looking Michael left, and Gabe returned his attention to her.

"So, Olivia, what am I to do with you, my vision from the future?" he teased.

HER ANSWER was prompt. "Help me find my car—uh, my horseless carriage. Maybe there's some kind of time warp surrounding it, and if I step back inside—"

She saw the incredulous look on his face and tried to circumvent it. "At least if we find the car, I can show you the book, the one with your picture."

He raised an eyebrow.

"The picture in that book is a copy of the portrait in your hallway," she told him. "At first, I couldn't believe it, but now I see it's true, and it makes everything fit together. This isn't a fantasy. There's a definite connection between what happened to me and that book."

"Oh, yes. I would like to see this mysterious book with my portrait in it."

"It's a reproduction, actually," she said, thinking ahead, wondering if she should tell him everything. So far, what she'd read in *Rogues Across Time* was true. Baron Northcliffe rode a large black horse and wore a black flowing cloak. The locals she'd met suspected he was the Highwayman; she was certain of it. But there was something else in the book, too. Something important.

"How old are you?" she asked.

"Eight and twenty. And you?"

"Twenty-six, but my age isn't important." She paused, calculating. His certainly was. But how did you tell a man that he was going to die—and soon?

"In the book—" She stopped midsentence.

"Yes? What else is in this book?"

"Your life—and death, Sir Gabriel," she added flatly. It was hardly the time to use his nickname. "You're going to be hanged, and soon. This year—1796."

Once again, he threw back his head and laughed. "Hanged, I? A peer of the realm? Do not be a fool, woman."

"Wait a minute," she cautioned. "I don't like being called a fool."

"How else can I react when you speak so absurdly?"

"I only know what I read," Liv said stubbornly. "I can't force you to believe me—"

"And what was the reason for my hanging? The insinuations that I am a murderer? I thought you did not believe those rumors." He was confused, wondering why she was trying to alarm him. Could all this talk of hers be a part of the plan his enemies had concocted?

"No, I don't believe you're a murderer," she replied. "But I *do* think you're the Highwayman. Whoever you are, you're going to be arrested—and hanged." Her voice trembled on the last word.

"I would like to see this book," he said slowly, thinking that perhaps he might learn more of his enemies' plot from it.

"Then take me to the place where you found me last night," she challenged.

Something was afoot, but he didn't know what. He did know, however, that she was very different from any woman he had ever met. It wasn't just the way she looked, her unusual height and great beauty. She was obviously a woman of intelligence and a quick mind, who knew of Shakespeare and never seemed at a loss for words.

But he could hardly believe that she was six-and-twenty. Women of that age were usually worn-out from childbearing, their skin had lost its softness and bloom and their teeth were often rotted and black. Olivia's skin was like porcelain and her teeth were white as pearls.

"Can you ride?" he asked abruptly.

"Ride? Oh, not very well. I haven't been on a horse in years. Except for last night, that is."

"Then we shall walk. It is no more than a mile. Are you up to it?"

She straightened her shoulders and held her head high. "Of course. I'm ready whenever you are."

"Then, Olivia, let us go and find this horseless carriage and the book that prophesies my death."

LIV TRAILED ALONG behind him across fields of green, but she couldn't get too excited about the surrounding countryside when her stomach was growling. Her last meal had been—how long ago? Breakfast before meeting Peggy yesterday morning—whenever that was. Of course, since then she'd traveled two hundred years backward—with nothing to eat except a slice of meat pie. And she was tired, too. This traveling through time was exhausting!

But it was hard to keep her sense of humor when there was no one to laugh with. So far, Sir Gabe seemed to be laughing *at* her. Meanwhile, he hiked on with rapid strides that she had trouble duplicating.

Admittedly, it wasn't a bad view from behind, watching the strong muscles of his calves and thighs as he walked, not to mention his rear end, which was made for those tight pants.

She shook her head and looked away. There was time for one thing only, finding her car and getting back— somehow—to her own century. He'd be a good memory, something to tell her friends in New York about, and then back in her own apartment she could fantasize about what might have been.

Hurrying to catch up, she looked around, hoping for a familiar landmark. But since she hadn't been able to see anything of her surroundings last night, she certainly wouldn't recognize the place today. She would have to depend on him to remember where he'd found her. That's where the car—and the book—would be.

As they reached the end of a path that turned into a rutted road, he announced, "Here we are."

Liv stopped and looked around, frantically searching the landscape for the ditch and the car.

"This is where I found you last night," he said. "I am not quite sure what your horseless carriage looks like, but I see no overturned conveyance of any sort."

Liv didn't, either. There was nothing on the road or anywhere around them. Just fields, wooded hills and a section of rock wall, partially collapsed.

"Are you sure this is the place?" she asked. "I don't remember the wall."

"I found you just here," he said, gesturing to the side of the road. I am rarely mistaken, especially about my own property. You were on *my* land, Olivia. I know every inch of it."

"But the wall—" She broke off uncertainly.

"It was the dark of night."

"I realize that," she said sharply as she approached the wall and climbed up on it, dislodging a few of the loose stones. At least from here, she could get a view of the surrounding countryside. In spite of his bragging, it certainly was possible that the baron had made a mistake.

She stood up on top of the wall, shading her eyes with her hand and turning slowly in a circle. If her car was anywhere around, she'd see it from here.

Tears glistened in her eyes. There was no car; it had vanished, and along with it the book that had brought her here. In the same way, her whole life had disappeared. She sank onto the wall, with her legs hanging off the side, and tried not to cry.

"Your horseless carriage is gone. And with it, I assume, the remarkable book that predicts my death."

Liv nodded wordlessly. It *was* a remarkable book. It had vanished and with it all hope of getting back to her own time.

"Do you happen to know the exact date of my demise? I would like to be prepared." His arm rested on the top stones, close to her knee, and a little smile played sardonically around his lips.

"I only know the year," she answered.

"Then I must wait," he said as the smile broke through.

Irritated at his teasing, she pushed him aside and started to clamber down. Because she was so determined to get off the wall with no help from him, she made a misstep, catching her foot on a loose stone. With a little cry, she realized she was falling.

He caught her but didn't set her on her feet. Instead, he held her tightly. His body was hard and lean against hers, and memories of their kiss in the library flooded hotly through her.

His eyes met hers, and once more she felt the connection between them. The moment was totally sensual as Gabriel let her slide slowly along his body until her feet touched the ground. She could tell by the curve of his lips and the gleam in his eyes that he was well aware of just how completely the intimacy affected her. He knew damn well that he turned her on.

Liv broke into laughter. Turned her on! Would he have any idea what she meant by that?

He released her and stepped back. "I see that you find the situation amusing, Olivia. Should I have allowed you to fall?"

"It's not that. It's everything. And it's not amusing, it's terrifying," she answered. "If I don't laugh, I'll cry."

He reached into his shirt pocket and pulled out a monogrammed silk handkerchief, which he offered to her.

She shook her head. "Thank you, but I'm not really going to cry." He stood before her, strong and sure and in control, his body blocking out the sun and casting a shadow over her. "Even you must admit that I'm in something of a predicament. Here I am with no money, no job, nowhere to live—" She sank onto a low place in the wall.

"You were a serving wench at the tavern—"

"Yes, I was, for a few hours. But I'm not going back there! Even if I wanted to, I doubt if Simon and Nora would have me. They thought I was insane. And they certainly didn't believe the time-travel story."

"Oh, yes, the time-travel story." Gabriel rubbed his chin thoughtfully. "I do not suppose you'll change that."

"No, I won't, because it's the truth, whether anyone believes it or not. I have no ties with this damned Haroldsgate place." She paused. "Except for you, of course."

"It always seems to come back to me, does it not?" He sat beside her on the wall.

She nodded.

"Then perhaps it is up to me to solve the problem." He slanted a dark-eyed look at her, studying her face intently. "Come back to Northcliffe Manor with me."

"Thanks, but I don't care to be a serving wench in any kitchen, yours included. That won't solve my problem."

"That is not what I had in mind, Olivia. I was thinking of something more personal . . ."

She turned the full force of her blue eyes on him. Her voice was icy. "Let's get something straight right now. I have no intention of becoming your kept woman."

There was the chuckle again, and this time it irritated her.

"What makes you think that is what I am suggesting?"

Color flooded her cheeks, but her answer was direct. "I'll tell you what. The way you held me just now.

The way you grabbed me and kissed me in the library. If you remember, I had to fight you off."

"Oh, yes, the kiss." He raised an eyebrow questioningly, touching his lips with his fingertip. She wondered what he remembered, the kiss—or the bite. "Do you think that I bed every woman I kiss?"

"I have no idea at all about your sexual habits."

He leaned close so that his breath tickled her ear. It was a heady feeling. She meant to move away from him, but she didn't. The warmth from his lips—and from his body—was hypnotic.

"But you are very curious?" He wrapped a piece of her thick hair playfully around his finger.

Liv pulled away. "I'm not at all curious about your sex life," she lied, her heart fluttering like the wings of a wild bird.

He stretched his long legs out in front of him, a pose that was so relaxed it seemed arrogant. "Allow me to explain myself, Olivia. First, you need to know that your defense of yourself with the letter opener, although charming and courageous, was unnecessary. I must emphasize that I only bed women who are eager and willing."

"And I assume there are dozens of those." She wished she hadn't said that, but she couldn't stop herself. Dammit, she was curious about him. And his women.

"Hundreds," he retorted.

She grinned despite herself. His sense of humor would fit perfectly in the twentieth century.

"And now for my proposition, if I may."

He took her silence as permission to go on. The game could be dangerous if she was indeed the spy he suspected her to be. But so far, he was playing it well.

"The proposition I am offering is a position within my household. Not as a serving wench or scullery maid, but as a personal lady's maid to my sister, the Lady Caroline."

"You have a sister?"

He growled a little under his breath. The woman had a way of testing anything he said. "I do. She has been with my aunt at Bath for a fortnight, but she returns today. Her own maid married and moved away."

"I know nothing about being a maid, and you know nothing about me—except that I might be crazy."

"To paraphrase Master Shakespeare, If you are mad, then there is method in it. This fantastical story of yours may be only a way for you to get close to me—for whatever reason." He watched carefully for her reaction.

"You are an arrogant bastard," she snapped. "Thinking everything revolves around you."

"Not arrogant. Just realistic," he answered. "Frankly, there is no better way to watch you than if you are at Northcliffe Manor. So, what is your answer, Olivia? A roof over your head and food on the table, or—"

"But could I make it as a lady's maid . . ."

"Caroline is not difficult to please. You will get along well, although perhaps she will not be as understanding as I about your strange journey back in time."

"Then I won't tell her about it—without your permission. I guess I won't be doing anything without *milord's* permission," she added sarcastically.

"See that you remember that." Laughter underlay his words, and then his voice became serious. "Caroline is very dear to me, and I expect her to be well taken care of. Any quarrel you have with me does not involve my sister."

Liv looked at him sharply. There was passion in his voice and an unspoken threat.

"I swear to you, I have nothing in mind but getting home. I miss my life. For your information, I had my own apartment in Manhattan and was heir to a farm in upstate New York. I had a good job, wore nice clothes and went to the theater and dined at the best restaurants. People depended on me—"

"You were an aristocrat?"

"No, just an average working woman. We did away with the aristocracy back in 1776."

"Ah, yes, your little revolution. We try not to dwell on that here in England," he said wryly.

"And now I'm 'here in England,'" she repeated, lifting her chin and squaring her shoulders, "I guess I'll have to deal with that." She paused. "From my position as your sister's maid."

"Then we are agreed." He reached for her hand and couldn't help noticing how soft and smooth it was. Serving wenches didn't have hands like these. But maybe spies did.

When her lips curved in a brave smile, he found himself smiling back at her. He wanted to reach out and touch her hair again, wrap his hands in its thick honey coils, let it trail across his face. He wanted to kiss away her fears and make her laugh with joy and pleasure. His heart beat with a slow, heavy rhythm, and he felt a tightness growing in his loins.

She fascinated him, and he was determined to have her, spy or not. The pleasures of making love to her would not dampen his suspicions. In fact, when they became lovers, she might, in a moment of passion, confess her part in the conspiracy against him.

Yes, he would bed her. There was a spark between them that her words of protest could not diminish. And all he had to do was fan the flame, and wait for the moment to be right.

"Come," he said, getting to his feet. "We will see what Cook has in the kitchen. After a good meal and a rest, who knows what the remainder of the day will bring."

"Anything is possible," Liv said, realizing that for a while, her life was out of her hands. "I came here in a millisecond of time. Maybe I'll leave the same way."

4

THREE HOURS LATER, her stomach filled with a meal of mutton and potatoes and her face washed from a bowl of cold water, Liv stood in the domed entrance hall with the other servants waiting for her ladyship's arrival. Glancing around, she felt amazingly compatible with the rest of the staff. Her skirt and blouse looked a little odd, maybe, but she had to giggle when she thought of what she could have been wearing. A miniskirt? Jeans? As it was, she was scrubbed clean, standing straight and serious, her hair tied back with a ribbon.

Two carriages had arrived. She'd glimpsed them through the wide front doors. And she could hear the stamp of horses' hooves, the clank of harness and a cacophony of voices: Gabe, a woman—obviously her new mistress—and another voice, slightly high-pitched but definitely male. Then the party swept into the manor.

Lady Caroline Stratton was petite, barely over five feet, Liv guessed. Her dark hair was drawn back from her face, but wayward curls managed to escape and cascaded around her cheeks. Her eyes were dark like her brother's, but hers were full of fun and sparkling with mischief. Her sprigged muslin dress was fitted tightly under the swell of her breasts and tied with a pale blue ribbon. A dark blue cape, short and embroidered with golden thread, swirled around her waist when she moved.

And Caroline moved constantly, gesturing, greeting the servants, chatting animatedly with her brother, taking off her big straw hat decorated with garden flowers and tossing it onto the hall table. She literally bubbled with life. Liv was reminded of a doll she'd once seen in an antique-store window on Second Avenue in New York. Porcelain complexion, wide dark eyes, rosebud mouth. Except this doll was too animated for any display case.

Liv was charmed.

Then the third person strode into the entrance hall, and Liv drew in her breath sharply. He was tall and slender, fashionably dressed in a light brown frock coat and buff-colored trousers. In one hand he carried a stovepipe hat, in the other a narrow, silver-topped cane. But his eyes, not his attire, held Liv's attention. She'd seen those eyes before, earlier that morning, when she'd almost been run down on the main street of Haroldsgate. He was the man in the carriage! He'd looked right at her and then disappeared behind the carriage curtain.

"Who is he?" she whispered to Cook.

"Viscount Tancred. Second cousin to the baron," came the answer. "He's arrived just in time to welcome her ladyship."

He must have heard the whisper, for he glanced their way, and his eyes met Liv's. She felt a cold shiver crawl along her spine. Quickly, she looked away.

After greeting each of the servants, Lady Caroline politely dismissed them except, of course, her new lady's maid. Not sure what she was supposed to do, Liv dipped up and down in numerous curtsies, aware of Gabe's amused eyes on her.

"Caro, this is your new maid, Olivia," he said with a raised eyebrow, adding, "I think you will find her most interesting."

"I am sure I shall, and thank you, dear brother, for engaging Olivia just in time for tomorrow's party." Caroline flashed Liv a dazzling smile. "Will you wait for the footmen to bring in my luggage, and then accompany it upstairs?"

Liv understood that the question was actually an order and responded appropriately, or tried to. "Yes, ma'am. I mean, mistress. I mean—"

"'Lady Caroline' will be sufficient, Olivia," Gabriel said as he took his sister's arm. "Come into the library for a moment, Caro. I have some letters to show you."

Liv bobbed a few more curtsies as Caroline and her brother went down the hall. Then she realized that the viscount hadn't followed them.

Instead, he stood by the sideboard where he'd placed his hat and cane. Slowly, he drew off his elegant pearl-gray gloves and put them beside his other belongings. All the while, his eyes were on Liv, so blatantly greedy that she felt ashamed beneath their gaze.

"Well, well, the new lady's maid. How convenient."

She headed toward the door, intent on following Caroline's instructions.

He moved quickly to block her path. "I was feeling a little lonely this evening, in need of...recreation," he drawled. "And here you are. Just in time."

Liv knew a line when she heard it, no matter the century. "I'm sorry, sir, but I'm Lady Caroline's maid, and that is my only obligation here at Northcliffe Manor."

She started to move around him, pleased at the ease with which she handled herself. Firm but not totally rude—as befit a lady's maid.

He didn't seem impressed. "I am a family member, wench, and our family always shares." He gave a wolfish smile and moved quickly to block her way again, reaching for her.

She sidestepped easily. "Don't even think about it, your lordship," she said, trying to combine a warning with semirespect. "There's no way you'll lay a hand on me."

An ugly look passed over the viscount's lean face. "I will not take such talk from a woman—especially a servant. I want a kiss now, wench. Tonight I will want much more. And, damnation, I shall have everything I want or you will feel my cane across your back."

There was a race for the door, and the viscount won. She almost bumped into him as he turned and raised his hand toward her. She didn't know whether his intent was to slap her or grab her, but her reaction was instinctive.

"Don't you touch me!" she shouted and pulled the can of pepper spray out of her pocket, aiming it at the viscount.

That's when she heard Gabe's welcome voice. "What in God's name is happening here?" he thundered, materializing out of the shadows of the hall like an avenging angel. "Jeremy Barton, control yourself. I will have no intimidation of my servants."

Liv slipped the spray back into her pocket and let out a shaky breath. "It's all right, your lordship," she managed to say. "I was handling the situation."

"And I shall end it now," he said between gritted teeth. "Go upstairs to her ladyship's rooms. My cousin will be leaving."

"But the luggage—"

"Go, I said."

His look was so fierce that Liv obeyed without arguing. She scurried up the winding staircase with Gabriel's sharp words echoing in her ears. Just before she closed the door to Caroline's rooms, she heard him say her name and then the word *wench*, followed by an angry response from Tancred.

She leaned against the closed door, her heart still racing. Tancred had unnerved her, but she could have handled him. She was thinking not of him, she realized, but of Gabriel. She felt strangely elated that her employer, once her rescuer, then her pursuer, was now her defender! And she, so recently at odds with him, couldn't help admitting the overpowering attraction she felt. The situation at Northcliffe Manor was becoming more bizarre—and fascinating—by the moment.

"YOU HAVE NEVER BEEN a lady's maid, have you?" Caroline asked the next evening as Liv struggled to pull the young woman's curls into a topknot.

"Well, let's put it this way," Liv answered, "this would be easier if I had some mousse or gel. Or even hair spray." At Caroline's frown, she quickly answered, "No, I've never been a lady's maid. Sorry that I'm doing such a poor job—" Just as she thought the hair was secured, it tumbled around Caroline's face again.

"Oh, it doesn't matter," Caroline said. "I can dress my own hair. All this maid business and being waited upon is silly, anyway. I think grown people should take care of themselves. And this evening, I shall officially be grown-up. I'm eighteen today," Caroline added, flashing her irresistible smile.

Liv dipped a curtsy and smiled back. "Happy Birthday, Lady Caroline."

"Thank you, Olivia." Caroline deftly twisted her hair into a classical Grecian knot, allowing a few beguiling wisps to curl around her face. "This is a very special night, and I want to look my best."

"You can't fail," Liv said sincerely. "Maybe I can help with your makeup." She looked through the items in Caroline's rosewood cosmetics box. She recognized rouge and powder but little else.

She looked up at Caroline's face reflected beside her in the beveled-glass mirror of the dressing table. "Though you hardly need any cosmetics at all."

"Cosmetics?"

Liv thought quickly and came up with another word. "Paint?" she tried hesitantly.

"Oh. I use very little paint." Caroline regarded herself with approval.

"Your skin is lovely without it."

Caroline smiled in thanks. "I avoid the sun and wash with cucumber water. And the world has changed, thank goodness. The days of those terrible powdered wigs are past. Although they still wear them at court, we here in the country are free from that curse. Ugh, how uncomfortable to have that huge mass on top of your head." She giggled. "I would probably teeter around like a spinning top!"

Liv joined in the young woman's laughter, totally enchanted with her.

"The French Revolution did bring some positive changes. A new freedom in dress—" Caroline looked at Liv, her eyes sparkling. "They say the French ladies wear no undergarments and dampen the fabric of their gowns so the outline of their breasts shows through. Have you ever heard of anything quite so decadent?"

Liv hesitated. She thought about X-rated movies, topless bars, strip shows—and thong bikinis. But she had the proper eighteenth-century answer. "No, milady, it's purely shocking. " Olivia fumbled in the box. "Rouge, perhaps?"

"Mmm, a little on my cheeks and lips." Caroline held still while Liv, feeling confident about her skills, applied the makeup. "Do you think I need powder?"

Liv opened the powder box. It was coarse, white and heavy. "Do you know the ingredients of this, my lady? Is it flour or rice powder?"

Caroline looked surprised. "I have no idea! What a strange question."

"I think we should skip the powder," Liv said firmly. "It might contain lead, and if it does, it could eventually poison you."

"Where on earth did you learn that?"

"Um, I read it somewhere. I just can't remember where, but it stuck in my mind. I know Queen Elizabeth used leaded powder . . . ."

Caro's dark eyes widened. "You can read? How wonderful. So few can. I tried to teach my last maid her letters, but she was not at all interested. Perhaps we can read to each other. Sometimes Northcliffe Manor is extremely boring." She lowered her voice. "I have a novel by Mr. Fielding. Of all his works, it is my favorite. But it is rather daring, and you must promise never to tell my brother that I am reading *Tom Jones*."

"Your secret is safe with me, Lady Caroline."

"Good. Now, about poisonous cosmetics, I *have* heard stories. A model, who sat for Reynolds years ago, died. But that was from mercury water, not powder—"

"Nevertheless . . ." Liv paused. Not sure *what* had happened *when*, she decided not to take any chances. "Why don't we forgo the powder—"

"I will be the only one without white skin . . ."

"Instead, your skin will be creamy, luscious and natural. Everyone else will look chalky-white." She waited a moment to let the words sink in. It worked.

"I will be the only one *without* white skin!" Caroline repeated, but this time the declaration indicated that she'd caught on. She gave Liv a hug. "I will be the only one! Oh, I am so pleased that my brother hired you. Now, for my dress. The gold one. It is in my armoire, I think."

Yes, it was in the armoire, as Liv well knew. She'd hung it there after spending hours that morning trying to iron out the wrinkles without success. The iron had to be heated in coals on the kitchen fire and then applied to the dress. Liv couldn't gauge the temperature and even though she used a damp pressing rag, she'd still managed to scorch a spot—fortunately, near the hem. The head maid, a large muscular woman, who had been watching scornfully, had snatched the iron from her and properly finished the task.

Liv helped Caroline slip the dress over her head and then closed the tiny buttons down the back of the high-waisted garment that was tied under the bustline with a purple satin ribbon. In the style of the day, the elbow-length sleeves were bound with the same color satin. She held the low-heeled satin shoes for the young woman to slip on and then helped her into the long white kid gloves.

She stood back and observed her mistress. "Jewelry? I wish I had my—" She broke off, thinking of the set of Victorian costume jewelry that was one of the showpieces of her design collection. The earrings and necklace in pearls and faux amethysts could have been made for Caroline.

The young woman lowered her voice conspiratorially. "I am not going to wear any jewelry because I think—oh, I hope—that I shall receive my grandmother's jewels tonight as a gift. Gabriel promised I could have them on my eighteenth birthday, and he never forgets a promise to me."

"Then I expect to see you bedazzled in jewels before the evening ends." As she helped button up the long gloves, Liv felt more like an older sister than a maid. Finally, she twirled Caroline around for one more look and pronounced her perfect. At that moment, there was a knock on the door.

She opened it, stared unabashedly, and let out a long, low whistle.

Gabriel lifted an amused eyebrow.

"Oh, you're gorgeous!" The words, like the whistle, came out before she could help herself.

She hadn't seen him since the day before, when she'd first been at odds with him and then defended by him. In the meantime, he'd certainly changed. From a casually dressed landowner, he had become a true lord of the manor in his midnight velvet frock coat and matching waistcoat.

He smiled and touched his white satin cravat as if to adjust it. "So, you approve, Olivia?"

She avoided giving more than a cursory glance at his skintight black breeches, but her gaze got caught on his muscular thighs.

She willed her eyes upward. His hair, pulled back into a queue, gleamed in the hallway's candlelight. That same light cast deep shadows across his face, adding to the aura of danger that shimmered around him. He was the sexiest, most handsome man she'd ever seen. She felt a rush of heated pleasure and excitement just being near him again. Liv swallowed hard and tried to remember his question.

A smile flickered across his lips. "I asked if you approve? Of my party attire, that is."

He was blatantly flirting with her. Very aware of Caroline's eyes on them, Liv managed to answer, "Indeed, sir." She curtsied, almost losing her balance and falling backward into a curio cabinet.

"Has my sister not told you that we Strattons rarely stand on ceremony, Olivia? You need not curtsy so constantly!"

Her response, programmed by now, was to curtsy again. "Damn," she muttered under her breath, straightening up quickly.

But he didn't hear her as he held out his hands to his sister. "Ah, Caro, you look elegant. So grown-up."

Caroline took his hands and blushed. "Thank you, Gabriel. I know the party is an expense we can scarce afford—"

"Don't be silly," he answered, taking her arm. "It is your eighteenth birthday. You deserve a party, and a party you shall have." He led her toward the door.

Caroline turned to Liv and to her surprise gave her a peck on the cheek. "Thank you, dear Olivia, for helping me. This will be the best night of my life."

"Have a wonderful time, your ladyship," Liv murmured, amazed by the stab of jealousy she felt that she wasn't on Gabriel's arm on her way to the party.

"Oh, Gabriel, one moment, please. I just remembered an instruction for Olivia." Caroline moved away from her brother and leaned forward, her dark curls touching Liv's face as she whispered, "If you wish to see the party, there is a spot in the south garden, near the fountain, that gives a good view through the windows."

Liv nodded, her earlier feelings of jealousy disappearing. If she couldn't be Cinderella and go to the ball, at least she would have a ringside seat.

SHE SLIPPED OUT through the kitchen, past several cooks preparing a late dinner for the party. Using the light of the moon, she made her way into the garden and located the fountain Caroline had mentioned, where marble swans spurted gurgling streams of water from their beaks. She pushed her way through the shrubbery, closer to the house, and let out a little sigh of pleasure. Floor-to-ceiling windows gave a perfect view of the party.

The door between two large formal parlors had been flung open and the rooms, lighted by hundreds of candles, glowed brilliantly. The candlelight concealed the run-down condition of Northcliffe Manor and turned the rooms into a kind of fairyland.

There was music and gaiety and laughter. And she was on the outside looking in—which brought back several unwanted memories.

She'd been a shy gangly teen, working in the diner while other kids went to parties and dances. In college—and afterward—she'd struggled to make herself into the new Liv Johnson, sophisticated and successful. She'd watched, listened and changed.

But in the eighteenth century, here she was again, not belonging. She might fantasize about being at the party, dancing with Gabriel, being held in his arms, but that part of the fairy tale would never come true.

Damn the powers that brought her to Northcliffe Manor as a maid, not a lady!

Well, she didn't need fairy tales, anyway. She needed common sense and intelligence to get home to the twentieth century. Plus a miracle. Of course, miracles *did* happen; her presence in the eighteenth century was proof of that. She smiled ruefully, thinking of *Rogues Across Time*, the book that started it all. *Rogue* was exactly the word to describe Gabriel.

What would happen next? Trouble, possibly. Whatever the baron was, Liv realized that she should keep her distance from him.

And she knew she wouldn't.

"I see you enjoy a gander at the gentry, too."

Liv whirled, startled to find Gabriel's steward beside her. "Michael! I'm embarrassed to be caught spying," she admitted.

"'Tis no shame, on such a night as this—a proud one at Northcliffe Manor. For tonight our Lady Caroline turns eighteen." He stepped closer and peered into the house. "Aye, she looks a bonnie lass tonight."

"Yes, she does," Liv agreed softly as she turned her eyes away from the festivities for a moment to have a look a Michael. She could see his face clearly in the light reflected through the windowpanes—and his eyes were fixed on Caroline. Like a lovesick pup, he watched the young woman move to the steps of an intricate dance, and his blue eyes danced with her. On his face was the expression of a man totally, desperately, in love.

"So that's how it goes," Liv whispered to herself.

"What?" Michael grudgingly turned away from the window.

"That dance, how does it go?" she asked, quickly covering.

"It's a gavotte, I believe, not that I've ever danced one."

"Neither have I." Together they peered back through the window. But while his attention was on Caroline, her eyes were searching for Gabriel. She saw him, not dancing, but standing alone at the edge of the crowd, his hands behind his back. She sighed. He was arrogant, mysterious and divinely handsome.

She remembered his arms around her, his kiss on her lips. *Dashing*, *handsome* and *devilish* were perfect words to describe him.

"On, I'd love to be inside!" she blurted out.

"Don't even think it," Michael said with a nervous chuckle. "That's not for the likes of us, Olivia. We're not of the upper classes."

"It doesn't have to be like that," she fumed. "In America, everyone is as good as anyone else. You ought to emigrate, Michael. You'd do so well where there are opportunities for bright, hardworking men like you."

"Nay, my girl, when I leave the Strattons, I won't be going to America. I'll be returning to my homeland, to Scotland. My father owns a fine piece of farmland, and someday it will be mine. I'm here just to learn—and to see a bit of the world."

"And to fall in love," Liv said in a low voice. "You do love her, don't you, Michael?"

"You ask too many questions, girl," he answered gruffly.

"Sorry."

They were quiet for a moment, listening to the music. A trio played, viola, violin and something that looked like a piano but sounded much tinnier.

With the music in the background, Michael finally answered her question. "Aye, I love her. Ever since she was twelve years of age and I taught her how to ride, darlin' Caroline has tickled my fancy. Aye, yes," he said, softly, almost to himself as he watched Caroline dancing. "'Till the mortal stroke shall lay me low, I'm thine, my Highland Lassie, O.'"

He turned to Liv with a wink.

She was curious. Where had she heard those words? Could Gabriel's steward be quoting poetry?

Michael, oblivious to her puzzlement, continued, "Indeed, she's a bonnie lassie, Lady Caroline. Good-hearted, too. Everyone in the county loves her."

"Yes, I'm sure they do," Liv answered, telling herself that Michael was just the romantic type, like most Scots, and spoke in a way that *seemed* poetic.

"That's why you see so many guests. Though I notice the viscount isn't among them. Good riddance, I say."

"Me, too," Liv agreed, remembering that she'd heard Gabriel order Tancred to leave Northcliffe Manor.

"Nary a one of the other fine guests would be here if 'twas only the baron entertaining."

"Why's that? Because of the rumors?" Liv lowered her voice. "About the Highwayman?"

"That and others," Michael said darkly. "The family's been plagued by gossip."

"Really?" She'd heard some of it in the tavern but wanted to know more.

"Aye. They say the old baron was a devil of a man himself. He was a hellion when he was young, and almost as mad as the king himself toward the end. His madness came from drink, they say. 'Twas a curse to him. But 'tis a good proud family," he concluded staunchly. "Some would have locked the old man away, but not Lady Caroline and the baron. Family is important to them."

"That's real loyalty," she said. "The baron and Caroline are very lucky. You're a good friend to them, Michael."

"And you are a very unusual servant, Olivia," he said, looking at her quizzically. She thought that he was pretty unusual, too, this poetry-spouting Scot. "Someday I'd like to hear your story and understand why the baron hired you." Michael smiled broadly. "Although I believe I know the answer to that."

A deep voice responded, seemingly out of nowhere. "Then you must be reading my mind, Michael."

The young steward jumped what seemed to Liv several feet at the sound of the male voice.

"Oh, no, sir. I would never presume to do that."

Gabriel stepped out of the shadows, a slight smile on his lips. "It would be a poor reading, anyhow, I expect." Before he finished the sentence, Michael bowed extravagantly, mumbled his apologies and disappeared down the garden path, leaving Liv alone with the baron. A ripple of excitement traveled along her skin and set her pulse racing.

He was *here*, beside her, no longer a fantasy. To her surprise and delight, he held out his hand. "There's a gazebo nearby. Would you like to walk with me?"

She let out her breath in a long sigh. "Yes," she whispered. How could she say no, when the moonlight was so bright and the air fragrant with the scent of flowers? And a dark handsome rogue was leading her—where? Into adventure, or so she let herself imagine.

His hand was warm on hers, and she felt her heart pound in a quick, staccato beat as he drew her along the graveled path. It was as if she were floating on moonlight. She didn't know why he had left the party to find her, and she didn't care. What mattered was that he was with her.

"Did you like what you saw of the party?" he asked.

"Yes, I—I'm sorry to spy on your guests."

"No, no, it is quite all right. I am happy that you enjoyed yourself. And the dancing, does that appeal to you?"

They climbed the steps of the gazebo. Liv walked to the railing and drew in a deep breath of heady summer air. "I love to dance. The gavotte is beyond me, I'm afraid, but . . ."

She turned toward him and let her voice drift off. Why not? she wondered. Part of her fantasy had come true. He was with her, and she might never have the chance again. "But I do know a dance we both might enjoy," she blurted out. "Are you willing to try? I dare you."

The baron's lips turned up in that familiar mocking smile, and his voice took on the smoothness of silk. "I never turn down a dare from a beautiful woman. However, we have no music."

"Oh, yes, we do, Sir Gabe. Be very still and quiet. Listen," she whispered. She expected to hear music waft toward them. "Hmm, I guess we're out of range. I'll sing. Or hum. I know a lot of tunes from the forties." She grinned up at him. "The 1940s, that is." She held out her hand and he took it. She felt giddy with triumphant excitement. "Now slip you arm around my waist."

She tossed her hair back in a gesture that fascinated Gabriel—alluring, provocative, maybe even dangerous. Her enemies could have coached her in the role of temptress, but if so, their trickery was playing into his desires because he was feeling a deep need for her.

She put her arm around his neck. "This dancing is going to be purely twentieth-century."

"So far, it is very appealing," he answered, chuckling softly. "I see you have quit fighting me, Olivia."

He saw a faint flush color her cheeks, but there was innocence in her voice. "A woman can change her mind. Even a serving wench."

Gabriel pulled her closer. "For tonight, you shall be a lady. Would you like that?"

"Very much. It's part of my fantasy—" She smiled. "Never mind, let's just dance."

"This dancing—is there more to it than standing, wrapped in each other's arms?" he asked. "Of course, this is most pleasurable—"

"Oh, we move. Like this, from side to side." She demonstrated. "Music will help."

She began to sing in a low husky voice. The song was about kisses and sighs and time going by. He'd never heard anything like it, neither the rhymes nor the melody.

He wasn't sure that he liked the song, but he very much liked her voice and her form of dancing, their bodies pressed against each other, her lush breasts brushing his chest, her thighs insinuating themselves between his. So tall and slim, she seemed to fit perfectly in his arms. But instead of producing an easy warmth between them, the dance created an inferno, so hot that even the night breeze couldn't cool it.

She was intent on her song, her forehead tucked against his shoulder, singing the words prettily.

"Did you write that yourself?"

She laughed up at him. "Nope, it's from *Casablanca*."

"Casablanca? You have traveled in North Africa?" He found her more fascinating by the moment.

Her blue eyes danced. "The movie *Casablanca*. Um, the film. Oh, damn. There's no way to explain this. It's a story you can *see*, a very romantic story of star-crossed lovers who can never be together. It's a movie, and movies mean nothing to you."

"But I do understand star-crossed lovers," he said softly, letting go of her hand and slipping his arm around her waist. He held her easily in his grasp, and she raised her face to his.

Her mouth was inches away, pink and inviting. Her body was here, now, pliant and warm, and he felt a sharp, eager pang of desire.

"Olivia, your schemes and subterfuges mean nothing when I'm holding you in my arms. I do not care who you are or where you are from. I have only one need that burns through me like a flame."

"Gabriel," she said desperately, "I don't know what's happening, why I'm here—or how long I'll be here. I only know that we have this moment in time . . ."

His voice was low and husky as he commanded, "Enough talk."

Then, suddenly his mouth covered hers, and she lost herself in the hungry, fierce kiss. Her blood sang in her veins like sweet hot wine, and her body ached with yearning. His tongue found hers, circled and sucked until she was dizzy with desire.

Not breaking the hot, moist contact of their mouths, she pressed closer to him, skating her tongue across his teeth, exploring the soft recesses of his mouth. When she heard his soft moan and felt his hips move against hers, Liv's skin flamed with heat and her heart beat wildly. She was out of control. She couldn't stop now. There was no need to, for this was just what she'd wanted when she asked him to dance. This kiss, so real, so believable—in a world that she couldn't believe at all.

When he finally tore his mouth from hers, his breath was hot against her ear. "I want you—now, Olivia," he said.

The hoarse sound of his voice only excited her more. Gasping, her head reeling from the powerful emotions that surged through her, she gazed up at him, so handsome, so dangerous. She was drawn to that danger, touching his face with her fingers. "I want you, too, Gabriel."

"We could make love here in the gazebo. I could pull up your skirts and take you like a peasant girl upon the ground." Then a rare smile lit up his face. "But not here, my Lady Olivia. You are no easy wench to be bedded so hastily. I want this night to be one that will live in our memories. Will you come to me in my bedchamber after the party?"

Liv's throat was too tight to speak.

"We shall share pleasure such as you have never known, Olivia." He kissed her once more, a tantalizing kiss, filled with promise. "Now, I must return to Caroline. I have a gift for her birthday."

"Yes, I know. This is a special night for Caroline—" Liv sagged back against the railing of the gazebo, her hand pressed to her swollen lips, talking of Caroline but thinking only of Gabriel—and herself. "And for us," she added.

He touched her hair gently. "Yes, for us also. Can you find my quarters?"

She nodded slowly. She didn't need to tell him that she'd already asked the second-floor maid where the baron slept and had walked by his rooms several times, plagued by curiosity about him.

He dropped a kiss on her cheek. "Until then, my Olivia."

As she watched him retreat along the garden path, Liv was reminded how often she'd been in this position, admiring his backside. This time, she wasn't fantasizing. Tonight, they would be together. She took a deep breath of night air. Crazy. Insane. She'd just made an assignation with an eighteenth-century man, whom history branded as a criminal.

She hugged herself tightly, gazed up at the moon and inhaled again, trying to calm herself. "It doesn't matter," she whispered to the starlit sky. "It's a miracle that we're together. If I turn away from him now, I'll regret it forever."

No regrets, she told herself as she walked back to the manor. When it was time to return to her century, if that time ever came, then she would go without wishing for what might have been.

LIV STARED at the small ormulu clock above Caroline's fireplace. What time did parties end at Northcliffe Manor? Did the guests dance all night, or would there be a midnight supper? She willed the clock's hands to move fast and time to pass. Not just because she wanted Gabriel so desperately, but also because if it didn't happen soon she might wake up to reality—and change her mind about going to his rooms.

"No," she murmured softly. She would never change her mind, even if she had to wait until dawn. His kiss lingered on her lips, and if she closed her eyes, she could still feel his hands warm and strong on her body. She had no more control over her feelings about Gabriel than she had about the adventure she'd been swept into. All she could do was follow her heart.

Finally, she heard Caroline's footsteps echoing in the hallway, and then the young woman burst into the room, her voice high and joyous. "Look, Olivia, look what Gabriel gave me—the jewels, just as I had hoped. Are they not beautiful?" She twirled in front of Liv, her dress billowing. Glittering at her throat and in her hair were a necklace and tiara of brilliant red and blue stones.

Liv caught her breath. "My God, they're fantastic!"

Caroline laughed musically. "Yes, they are the Stratton jewels—rubies and sapphires."

"They must be worth a fortune."

"So everyone says," Caroline agreed airily. "But now they are mine. I am going to sleep in them tonight!" Her cheeks were flushed, and her eyes sparkled.

"They should be locked in a safe," Liv warned.

"Gabriel said the same, but I begged him to let me wear them tonight—all night. Tomorrow he will lock them away again." She pulled a rueful face. "He says I must be very careful how I display them. He did not give them to me with my other gifts. I was so nervous, thinking that I would not get the jewels tonight—or ever. Then, when all the guests had left, and we were alone, he gave me the box with these inside."

"You're really going to sleep with them?" Liv's fingers were itching to get her hands on the jewelry. She'd done some work with precious stones, resetting old rings and bracelets into new designs, but she'd never seen anything like Caroline's jewels, neither in size nor quality.

"Oh, I guess not. That would really be silly. But I will keep them on for a little while, until I am ready for bed."

After a cup of hot milk brought in by a sleepy kitchen maid, Caroline let Liv help her undress and slip into her long white cotton nightgown. Still wearing the jewels, she climbed into her bed.

Liv puffed the pillow up around her, smiling down at the young woman who looked more like a doll than ever with her dark curls, dancing black eyes—and sparking jewels.

"I guess it is time for you to lock them away," she said, reluctantly unclasping her necklace and removing the tiara. "Please put them in the drawer of my dressing table, and I shall sleep with the key under my pillow."

Liv nodded and accepted the jewels. As she walked to the dressing table, she weighed them expertly in her hands and realized they were very light. They should be heavier, more dense. But the colors—good and clear. Just to be sure . . .

There was a candelabra on the dressing table, and she held the necklace and tiara close to the flickering light. Without a loupe for careful study, she tried to analyze them quickly. Intent on examining the jewels, she didn't even hear Caroline's question.

"Olivia!"

"Yes?"

Caroline laughed. "I understand why you are so entranced. They are wonderful, are they not?"

"Extraordinary." Slowly, almost as if in a daze Liv put the jewels in the drawer, locked it and gave the key to Caroline.

"Thank you, Olivia." She tucked the key beneath her pillow, as promised, and with a sigh, sank back on the soft goose-down pillows. "This has been the best night of my life."

"I'm so happy for you."

"Do you think my dreams will be wonderful, too?"

"I'm sure they will be."

Caroline smiled sweetly. "Please close the bed curtains and blow out the candles."

"Yes, Lady Caroline." Liv started to curtsy and then remembered the reprimand she'd been given by Gabriel. So much curtsying wasn't necessary here at Northcliffe Manor. It didn't matter, anyway, because Caroline, the sweet smile still on her lips, was already asleep.

Liv unloosened the heavy curtains that enclosed the huge four-poster bed and blew out the candles on the bedside table and in the candelabra. When she got to the door, Liv realized that she was shaking, not with excitement but with rage and disgust. She closed Caroline's door behind her and turned down the long shadowy hall toward the baron's room. Oh, she'd visit him, all right. And it would be a visit he'd never forget.

5

LIV THREW OPEN the door to Gabriel's rooms and took in the scene. The baron was standing near the bed, framed in the soft glow of candlelight. His frock coat, waistcoat and cravat were tossed over a chair, his shoes and stockings on the floor.

Charging in, she stopped long enough to see the whole man, unbuttoned shirt and all. He was in the process of removing the shirt, and she watched unabashedly, her eyes widening at the sight of his broad chest, bare, gleaming and bronzed. For a moment, an overwhelming urge of longing overcame her anger. Then she remembered Caroline.

Slamming the heavy oak door behind her, she accused, "You arrogant bastard!"

"Olivia, what—"

"It's one thing to play this ridiculous highwayman role, riding out and robbing from the rich, but quite another to steal from your own sister." Her voice rose an octave.

"Stop this screeching, woman."

"Your own *sister*," she emphasized, "who adores you."

"Lower your voice," he demanded, crossing the room in two long strides and reaching for her.

Liv stood her ground as his large hand wrapped

around her wrist. She should have been afraid, but she wasn't. Anger prevailed.

"What in the name of all that's holy is this about?"

"It's about the fake jewels in the necklace and tiara," she responded furiously. "It's about deception. It's about your sister's belief that she has the precious Stratton jewels, when all she has is paste."

Gabriel glowered back at her, but he was undeniably stunned. Dear Lord, he thought, this woman was full of surprises.

Her head was held defiantly and her blue eyes met his fearlessly. "How could you deceive someone who loves you as she does?" When he didn't answer, she continued, "You can't deny the deception. The jewels are fake. I know that because I'm a professional jeweler."

He was filled with admiration for her spirit and irritation for her interfering nature. Especially when all he'd wanted was to bed her...

He released her arm and walked over to the sideboard, allowing himself a moment to recover before pouring two glasses of port from the decanter. He handed her one and then picked up the other, wondering how much he should tell her.

She held her glass without drinking and regarded him coolly. "I'm waiting, Baron."

Enough to placate her, he decided, but no more. "My father replaced the real jewels with paste." His words were flat and direct. "He lost the Stratton rubies and sapphires in a card game which Caroline knew nothing about. My intent was to get the original jewels back. I was abroad—on the continent—at the time, but I had always hoped to return the jewels to their settings before Caroline's birthday." His jaw tightened. "I did not succeed."

Liv drained the glass of port in two gulps and set it down on the sideboard with a resounding thump. He'd never seen a woman drink like that before and could only stare at her, unbelieving.

She returned his gaze. "So. You ride as the Highwayman, hoping to steal back the Stratton jewels. Maybe you don't even know who has them, but you probably have a good idea. Someone in the nobility," she speculated, watching him carefully. "I'm right, aren't I?"

Gabriel cursed under his breath. Bloody hell, she was smart. But he was smarter. She wasn't going to trick him into talking about the Highwayman—and then reporting everything he said to his enemies.

Deliberately, he changed the subject. "What are you going to tell my sister?"

"About the fake jewels? Nothing, of course. Why should I hurt her? Go ahead and lock them up again tomorrow and keep on fooling her. But someday she'll find out, whether from you or someone else. Then she'll hate you for lying to her. And that's not all." She stopped to catch her breath before charging on. "Eventually, she'll learn that you ride as the Highwayman. A fact that I know for certain because I read all about you in that book. You can fool her, at least for a while, but you can't fool me at all."

"My dear, I have no intention of fooling you." He put his empty glass beside hers on the sideboard and then gave a little push until the two glasses touched. He paused dramatically and looked across at her. "Because I have other plans for us." He took a slow, steady step toward her.

Liv's blue eyes widened. "You don't expect—I mean, you don't think we're going to . . . Not after this!"

"I want you as much now as I did in the garden. No, that's not true," he corrected, his eyes boring into hers. "I want you *more* now than I did then, despite your interfering, trickery and spying."

"Spying? You think I'm a spy?"

"Tonight it does not matter what I think, only what I feel."

His heart was pounding at an irrational rate. Just touching her did that to him. The hot blood of desire roared in his ears. If she was his enemy, what matter? Let the devil be damned! He wanted her, and he would have her. He pulled her toward him and slanted his mouth across hers. "Just one kiss, Olivia. Just one, and then . . ."

Liv struggled for a moment, but the familiar heat, the strength of his arms, the hard muscles of his chest, triggered reactions she couldn't control. His touch hummed through her and heated her senses. Before she realized what she was doing, she'd reached up and loosened the ribbon that held his queue. His dark hair fell forward around his face. She entwined her hands in it as she opened her mouth under his.

Their breaths mingled hotly, and she moaned against his lips, tasting him. She wanted him desperately, Highwayman or not. It didn't matter. Nothing mattered but his mouth on hers, his body against hers, his heat melding with hers.

Once more, her hands seemed to be acting on their own as she reached inside his open shirt and ran her fingers across his bare chest. His skin was warm and pliant, his nipples hard and taut beneath her hands. It excited her to feel this man from another century react so passionately to her touch. She slid her hands around his body, raked her fingernails down his back and glowed with satisfaction as he grew tense and pressed closer to her.

"Vixen," he said in a voice low, husky and full of need. "You are all woman, totally and provocatively."

She smiled at the overblown compliment. "And you, my beautiful Gabriel, are all man. Thank God for that," she added.

He drew back, just enough to slip his hands between them and fumble with the buttons of her blouse. Unsuccessful and frustrated, he tore the blouse open. The sound of the ripping cloth sent chills along her spine. In this now-or-never relationship, anything could happen.

Before he could tear off her skirt, she quickly unzipped it, watching the look of amazement of his face. Of course! She realized that he'd never seen a zipper. She pulled off the skirt and tossed it aside with the blouse. Then before she could straighten up, he leaned over and swept her into his arms.

His bed was only steps away, but because this was her fantasy, he carried her. It *was* a fantasy, she told herself, an incredible flight into another century. Yet now it was real. She felt his hands on her skin. Feelings this potent couldn't be a dream.

He settled her on the bed and leaned over her, his hands hungrily caressing her body. As he cupped her breasts, attempting to pull away the lacy bra, Liv knew that he was encountering something utterly foreign to him, a woman in twentieth-century lingerie.

"Damnation," he murmured. "What is this garment that keeps you from me? Never have I seen lace so confining." He tugged at the straps.

"It's a brassiere. The hooks are in the back."

"A *brazier?*"

"Never mind. Just get the damn thing off me."

Gabriel found the hooks and pulled off the lacy bra. He paused, devouring her with his hot fiery gaze, and then he touched her breasts, lingeringly, with both hands. But she wasn't completely naked yet. "And this?" he asked, tugging at the waistband of her panty hose.

"Take them off, too. I'll explain later." She kicked away her boots and then helped him tug the panty hose down her hips and thighs—and onto the floor. Now, at last, she was ready for him.

He looked down at her, perplexed. Who was she, this wonderful creature who ensnared him with her wiles—just as she did with all those mysterious garments? It didn't matter now. His desire overpowered his curiosity. He'd promised Olivia a night to remember, but need for her was raging in him like a fever. As he removed his shirt, Gabriel vowed to hold his own desire in check and pleasure her with his hands and mouth until she begged for sweet release.

Lying beside her on the bed, he took her in his arms and kissed her, first her mouth, her chin, the slim line of her throat, and then the soft hollow between her breasts. Her eyes were closed, and she let out a long, tremulous sigh as he took her nipple in his mouth. His tongue circled the taut pink orb, and his lips sucked possessively. With her head flung back, she arched toward him as if to offer her body for his further exploration. She was his exotic delicacy, and he moved his mouth from her breast down along her abdomen and across her hipbone, tasting all of her.

His tongue was warm against her skin, and Liv held her breath . . . waiting. She felt his slow and deliberate touch on the softness between her legs. He caressed her with his mouth and tongue. Moist dark heat rose inside her, engulfing her. She wondered if it were possible to die from pleasure.

Just when her aching need seemed more than she could bear, he was beside her, kissing her eyes, her nose, and then her mouth. All she could think of was becoming part of him. She reached for his waistband and together—with shaky, eager hands—they stripped off his breeches.

She ran her hands along his smooth, moist skin, down his lean hips to his strong, muscled thighs. She felt his heat all along her body, masculine, powerful, all-encompassing.

She murmured against his mouth, "I knew you'd be naked under those tight pants."

"You talk too much," he answered, his voice low and hoarse.

"No more talk, I promise." She touched his manhood, caressed the long, hard length of his erection and heard his gasp of pleasure as she fondled him. He brought his lips down on hers, kissing her hungrily, filling her mouth with his tongue.

He pulled her to him, so close that she could barely get her breath.

And then he entered her.

Liv gasped at the wonderful fullness, a long shuddering sigh that left her trembling in his arms. He moved inside her with powerful unrestrained thrusts that brought her quickly to the edge of her climax. She tried to hold on to the moment, but he pushed her further into a long ever-deepening spiral of passion in which they moved in perfect rhythm.

The pressure built and twisted inside her, and she lifted her hips, clutching with her hands and arms, wrapping her legs around him.

Her instinctively provocative movement lit the final fire within Gabriel. There was nothing in his world but Olivia and the intensity of pleasure she gave him. No longer able to control the passions that drove him, his convulsive explosion of release shook him to the core of his being.

Olivia clung to him. Wave after wave of pleasure rocked her, and she thought her heart would burst and take her breath from her body. She dug her nails into his moist, slick shoulders and cried out her joy and triumph.

THEY LAY wrapped in each other's arms in the huge four-poster bed. The candles had gone out and the room was thrown into total darkness. For Liv, that only added to the erotic fantasy she was experiencing. Where was she, really? In another country, another century—or in a dream? Suddenly, it didn't matter, as long as she was with Gabriel.

She ran her fingers from his lips to his shoulder, down along his chest, the curve of his waist, to his hip. His body was marvelous, muscular and hard without an ounce of fat. A twentieth-century man would pay a fortune to a health club or personal trainer to develop a body half as wonderful as Gabe's.

He lay beside her, reveling in the touch of her fingers. Never before had he lain with a woman like this, after lovemaking, and felt so at ease, so wrapped in warmth and caring. Even stranger, he wanted to talk to her, laugh with her, hug her close.

He moved his hands along her body, stroking her hips, cupping her bottom, imitating her own caresses. Even tickling her ribs.

She giggled aloud, and when he changed his tickles to soft strokes, she purred with satisfaction. "You are something, Gabe Stratton, Baron Northcliffe." She loved saying his name, rolling his title off her tongue.

"Not 'Sir Gabe'?" he teased.

"No, just 'Gabe.' It's more familiar. And right now, I feel *very* familiar," she added. What could be more difficult to believe, she wondered—that she was sleeping with a baron whom she called Gabe or that it was happening in the eighteenth century? "Yes, you're something else, Gabe."

"And you are . . . something else, too," he repeated, not sounding sure about the expression. "Not only a vixen, but a wildcat in bed. My back will bear your scratches for a week."

Liv was contrite. "Oh, I'm sorry. I can kiss them and make them better."

Gabriel chuckled. "Later, perhaps, but now there are other parts of my body I would like for you to kiss."

Liv rolled on top of him. "Your wish is my command, milord. For once, I think I'll listen to what you have to say."

"YOU'RE NOT ASLEEP, are you?" She gave his shoulder a shake.

"Of course not, only resting to regain my strength."

He pulled her into the curve of his body. "Any other time, I would be asleep now, alone in my bed, not even thinking of what had happened during the night. But not with you, my Olivia. There are many reasons not to sleep, many things to occupy the hours of darkness."

"Those other times, with other women . . ." She hesitated briefly, but she had to know. "Were there many?"

"Of course," he said, followed by a low laugh. "Not so many, after all, and certainly none like my woman from another time."

Liv relaxed against him, feeling his warm breath on her skin. She slipped her arm around his chest and rested her head against his shoulder, snuggling closer. The dreamy afterglow of lovemaking still enveloped her and wrapped her in a sensual web.

"Oh, Gabriel, this is so . . . so unreal. And wonderful," she added. "I'll remember this night forever."

"There will be other nights more memorable than this one. Tomorrow night, and the next and the next—"

"You mean that you're not simply the lord of the manor bedding his serving wench—and then forgetting her?" She tried to make her voice light, but the question was a serious one that had been hovering like a dark shadow at the edge of her happiness. At first, she'd wanted just the moment. But now, after being with him so completely, things were different.

"I told you, Olivia, this is an evening unlike any other. I shall not forget it. Not for a moment. And I expect to repeat it often." He chuckled. "You have invaded my life as our Henry the Fifth did France. Besides, I need to keep my eye on you," he teased.

"You still believe I'm a spy sent by your enemies? After what happened between us tonight?"

She felt him shrug his shoulders in the darkness. "Perhaps you have intentionally used your delectable feminine wiles to cloud my brain."

"Oh, of course I have," she said with a giggle. "But my mind is clouded, too. And my senses reeling, and my head—anyhow, you understand. I'm not a spy, Gabriel, but I still believe you're the Highwayman."

"Believe that if you will, Olivia. Some even think that I strangle beautiful young women on the Downs."

"No, they're wrong. I don't believe that at all. It doesn't make sense with what I know of you. But someone is a killer." She fought back a shiver." Surely you have suspicions."

His voice was cold. "I know more than one man evil enough to do such deeds, but mere speculation is not enough to lay the rumors about me to rest. I need real evidence." Gabriel swung his feet from the bed and pushed aside the heavy curtains. She heard him hit the floor and curse when his toe came in contact with the bedpost. He stumbled around in the darkness and opened the door.

"Carson," he bellowed. "Bring up some food from the kitchen and fetch me a candle—now!"

Liv pushed her hair back from her eyes, scooted to the edge of the big bed and peeked out between the heavy curtains. Gabriel was framed by the light of long, burning tapers from the hallway as he struggled into a damask robe. She saw the shadow of a man listening as Gabriel gave him a brief order. Then Gabriel shut the door.

"You're changing the subject with food," Liv suggested.

"Not at all." He turned to the sideboard and poured another glass of port. "But I thought we could both do with a bit of nourishment."

"Well, you're right about that." She looked around for something to cover herself. His shirt was on the carpet near the bed. She picked it up and slipped it over her head. The fabric was cool and soft against her heated skin. And it smelled deliciously of him. She hugged her arms around herself and looked up at him as he sipped port in his elegant robe.

"It must be nice to have servants attending you night and day," she murmured.

"I never think of it. Nor does the night porter. It is his job, and I expect he feels lucky to have it."

"I wasn't criticizing, only commenting." She padded across the floor and held out an empty glass, which Gabriel silently filled. "It takes a lot of money to run this place, doesn't it?"

"Yes, it does. Fifty rooms, gardens, grounds—"

"Not to mention your stables," she added.

Gabriel downed the port, sank into a high-back chair, his robe loosely belted, and stretched out his long legs. "Hardly 'keep up,' Olivia. Michael and I are rebuilding from almost nothing. My father was robbed not only of my sister's dowry—the family jewels—but some of our finest horses." Gabriel paused for a long moment, and she waited, not willing to probe at this point.

Finally, he went on, "When I was abroad at school, they lured him into their gambling circle. A scheming group of noblemen, so-called, they took advantage of his weakness. Livingstone, Cardiff, Fremont and the rest, damn them all—" He broke off warily. "I talk too much."

"No, please, tell me. Why did you go away at such a time?"

"I had no choice. My father sent me to the continent. His companions insisted that it would make a man of me to travel abroad. In fact, it was simply a scheme on their part to get me out of the way. But one he was happy to comply with. He wanted to drink and gamble without censure. By the time I returned, everything was lost."

She managed to remain quiet for a little while, knowing she should let the subject drop. But when he moved aside for her to settle by him in the chair, she slipped in a question. "Is it so important to get it all back—the money, the horses, the jewels..." She watched him consider that. "Maybe you would have been happier with less."

Still contemplating what she'd said, he raised an eyebrow wryly. "You are right, my Olivia. I could be satisfied with much less. No horses, except for transportation, no money for repairs and upkeep on this massive heap of stone." He gestured around the shadowy room. "Not even a dowry of jewels for my sister." He slipped his arm around her waist. "But you must understand that this is not my decision."

She saw his jaw tighten and looked at him questioningly.

"I am Baron Northcliffe. This land has been passed down for centuries, back to the first land grant from Henry the Eighth. I can't turn my back on Northcliffe Manor. It must be kept whole for my children's children. Its stable must be maintained and brought into the winner's circle once more." He smiled down at her. "And I am determined to see the family jewels returned for Caroline to provide a suitable dowry. My sister is all that is left of my family."

"There is your cousin, Viscount—"

Gabriel grimaced. "A far-removed relative, but one who has turned covetous eyes toward Northcliffe Manor. He is next in line to inherit the estate and the title."

"But he's only a cousin. What about Caroline?"

"The estate is entailed for males of the line. My sister can never own Northcliffe Manor."

Liv sighed. Two hundred years made a lot of difference! "You're trapped, aren't you? If you give up this house, the land and horses—and the jewels—then you give up hundreds of years of history and tradition."

He looked deeply into her eyes and realized that she knew him as no one ever had. "That would be like turning my back on my family. I could never do that. You understand, don't you?"

"Yes, I do."

He readjusted himself in the chair and settled her in his lap. "I believe you truly do, Olivia." He kissed her softly, smoothing back her hair.

"It's because I feel the same as you. About my ancestral home." She laughed softly. "It hasn't been there for centuries, just since my grandparents bought the land and built the house, maybe fifty years ago. Which would actually be a hundred and fifty years in the future, but never mind that! I inherited it, even though I'm a woman. Things are different in my century, thank heavens. At first, I thought about selling—"

"Selling your family land?" His voice resonated with surprise.

"It would have been the sensible thing to do. But I've learned that I'm not always sensible. Sometimes it's best to take chances. Like tonight." She kissed him lightly on the lips. "I'm definitely going to keep it—if I ever see the place again."

"The place," he repeated with a puzzled frown, "which is in America—"

"Yes. But America two hundred years from now. I know, you still don't believe I come from another time and place, and I can't think of any way to convince you. If only I'd brought some photographs with me."

"Photo-graphs?"

She laughed. "Of course, I'd have to explain what they were!" She leaned against him, shaking her head. "I wish there were something I could invent, like a light bulb or something..." At that, she sat up straight in his lap, so abruptly that he tightened his arms to keep her from tumbling onto the floor. "I wonder if Ben Franklin has flown the kite yet?"

"Benjamin Franklin, the diplomat from America?"

"Yes! You've heard of him?"

"Of course, he was very popular in France. A little less so here."

"Did you ever hear about his discovering electricity?"

Gabriel frowned and shook his head.

"Hmm. Maybe he hasn't done it yet."

"If he has not, then he never will, Olivia. He's been dead for several years!"

"Really? Are you sure?"

"There you go again, testing me. Yes, I learned of his death when I was on the continent."

"I always was terrible with dates." She leaned back again. "There has to be some way to convince you that I'm not a spy. I'll think of something," she said determinedly. "But I do wish I had a photograph of my farm. Oh, Gabriel, it's so beautiful, with rolling hills and massive trees and green pastures." She stopped and smiled. "It's very much like your land, now that I think about it. Except there're no horses on the farm now."

"Then how do you travel? Oh, yes," he answered his own question. "Your horseless carriage!"

"That's right, you're learning," she teased. "But there once were horses on the farm, when my grandfather had his stables. He boarded them for other people—and raised a few of his own."

Gabriel's eyes brightened. "Thoroughbreds?"

She laughed. "Hardly. But the Saratoga racetrack was only a couple of hours away. My grandfather always dreamed of racing a winner there. But it never happened."

"Then you appreciate fine racing horses?"

"I could learn to," she said softly, leaning forward to kiss his cheek. For this man, she thought, she could learn anything. To live in the eighteenth century. Even to love a highwayman.

"Michael will help you. And so will Caroline. She's a fine horsewoman—"

She nuzzled her head against his neck. "Do ladies' maids ride with the nobility?"

"At Northcliffe Manor, they do, if I wish it. After all, I make the rules and establish the customs for others to follow. In any case, Caroline would enjoy your company as a riding companion." He stroked her hair. "And I enjoy your company for so many reasons." He slipped one hand beneath the shirt, his fingers teasing her nipple.

Liv felt a deep wave of desire wash over her. "I told you I wasn't going to be your kept woman. Remember?" It was difficult to keep her voice steady when his fingers were so skillfully satisfying. Their touch caused her skin to tingle and her blood to turn warm and thick, like melting honey.

"I am not keeping you, dear Olivia," he teased. "You are free to leave my bed."

She touched his face, moved her fingers across the faint bristling of whiskers, traced the outline of his lips with her fingertip and caressed the silkiness of his hair.

"I don't want to leave your bed," she whispered. "And I never want to leave you." She was surprised at herself for the passion and truth in her voice. In fact, she couldn't bear the thought of leaving him. "Besides, we have to keep our eyes on each other," she joked. But there was no lightness in her voice when she added, "If we're not together, the centuries might separate us again."

"We will be together, my Olivia. You will stay here with me." His arms closed tightly around her, and his lips found hers.

There was a faint knock on the door.

"Your servant," she murmured through the kiss. "The food . . ."

"It can wait. For this moment, I have another appetite that must be fed."

"But—"

"Don't worry, Olivia. He will leave the dinner outside my door so that we can indulge ourselves later. For now—"

Liv had already started to shrug off the shirt and pull open Gabriel's robe. She trembled with desire and need as bare skin touched bare skin. Her heart skittered wildly in her chest. Her fingers found the hardness of his manhood, stroked, caressed.

As if their moves were choreographed, Gabriel shifted Olivia in his lap, and she straddled his thighs, her knees on each side of his hips. He lifted himself toward her and she settled on him, crying out in pleasure as she gave herself totally to the madness of the moment, forgetting everything but her lover and all the wonderful things he was doing to her.

6

A FULL MOON CAST its silver sheen along the twisting, winding road. From his carefully chosen position among the shadow of the trees, the rider watched.

He liked the inky darkness of night with only the moonlight as his guide. It heightened his sense of recklessness and danger. And yet there was something aesthetic about it, too, with the scents of summer carried upon the soft breeze.

His horse stamped nervously, shaking his great head and whinnying softly. The rider bent low and ran his hand gently along his mount's neck. "I hear it, too, old fellow." It was the sound of a carriage approaching, a team of horses, their hooves pounding the earth, their traces rattling and clanking.

He pulled down a black hood with slits for his eyes and mouth. It completely concealed his identity and gave him the spectral look of something otherworldly. He knew that, and it amused him immensely, even now, only moments before the deed was to be done.

The thrum of hooves along the hard-packed road stopped him in his musings and caused his heartbeat to accelerate. It was almost time. Excitement built, slowly, and then more rapidly until it raced through him with the fire of heady French brandy.

"May the gods of good fortune ride with me this night," he whispered into the wind.

Then he dug his heels into his stallion's flanks, and with a bound the great steed was off and running, out of the trees, down the hillside toward the road. He leaned forward in the saddle, low over his mount's neck, and his great cloak blew behind him like a dark cloud.

Too late, the coachman saw the black figure approaching. Frantically, he whipped his team and shouted at them to move faster, but the Highwayman gained, yard by yard. Within moments, the chase was ended.

LIV AND CAROLINE walked along a gravel path overlooking the gardens, carrying damask-covered pillows. Along the way, a bubbly Caroline pointed out her favorite flower.

"Just look, Olivia, how unusual, like little hearts in a bell. And the vivid colors! Have you ever seen anything like it?"

"Yes, it's my favorite," Liv said.

"Where do you know it from?"

"Oh, those have been my favorite flowers since I was a child."

"That is impossible," Caroline declared, clutching Liv's hand. "They are new flowers, only recently brought into the parish."

"Well, I'm not from here, you see," Liv explained. She'd told Caroline nothing of her background, and although the young woman must have wondered about her strange accent, she'd asked no questions of her lady's maid. To do so, Liv suspected, would have been considered unseemly.

"Even so, you could not have known about that flower as a child because it has only come to the country in recent years." She laughed infectiously. "Perhaps you dreamed it."

"Perhaps so," Liv agreed, not anxious to get into the details of her background with Caroline, as she'd done on numerous occasions with the young woman's brother.

They followed the path to a partially shaded hillock and put their pillows on a marble bench, which they shared, settling comfortably, Caroline with her embroidery, Liv with her book. It soon became evident that Caroline was more in the mood for gossip.

As she prattled on about the most recent news gathered after the church services that morning, Liv finally put down her book. But she still listened halfheartedly, her concentration not on Caroline but on her brother. She couldn't get him out of her mind—and didn't want to.

Over the past week, she'd left his bed in the mornings and spent the rest of the day longing for darkness and the warmth of his body next to hers. To her delight, he'd managed to come up with all sorts of excuses to get her away from her lady's maid role at various times during the day. She warned that someone would see him. He reminded her, again, that at Northcliffe Manor he made the rules for others to follow.

So she met him when and where he suggested. She was obsessed, lost in her world of fantasy.

She sighed and sat up a little straighter, acting the role Gabe had chosen for her, as his sister's maid, even if she didn't quite look it in the skirt and blouse that had been altered for her and served as a sort of uniform. But anything beat what was left of her own blouse, which Gabe's eager hands had left in tatters. It was now folded away in a drawer with her twentieth-century skirt.

Her uniform wasn't a perfect fit. Liv was a little above average height in her century, but in this one, she was gigantic. Even the men were shorter than she was. Except for Gabe, who was really the only one who mattered.

Trying to put Gabe out of her mind, she caught Caroline's last sentence.

"Of course, the Prince of Wales is in love with a married woman. I feel so sorry for his wife."

Liv turned to her mistress, startled. "Princess Diana? Prince Charles?" No, wait, she told herself. Caroline couldn't know anything about those twentieth-century royals!

Caroline put down her embroidery. "No, Olivia. Prince George and Princess Caroline of Brunswick. Everyone knows that."

"Of course," Liv said. "Sometimes I get confused."

Caroline leaned forward, her voice a whisper. "Surely you know that the prince has loved her for years."

"The princess?"

"Certainly not, the married woman. Maria Fitzherbert. He was even married to her once, but the king put an end to it. You must know all this. The servants gossip about the royals, too, don't they?"

"Oh, yes," Liv said quickly.

"So you know all that happened before King George the Third became *totally* mad. But mad or not, he was right. Royalty cannot marry a commoner. Indeed, it is not done."

Liv let out a chortle. "Oh, that will change someday, Lady Caroline. I guarantee it."

Caroline frowned. "You sound so certain. How can you know?"

"Trust me," Liv said firmly. "Someday a woman will be able to marry the man she loves, regardless of his status. Or hers."

A fleeting look of longing passed over Caroline's face. "I wish that were true. For if it were..." Her voice trailed off.

"You would marry Michael?" Liv blurted out without thinking.

Caroline drew her shoulders up stiffly. "Olivia! That is very bold of you to suggest."

"Please forgive my stepping out of line, Lady Caroline," Liv said.

Caroline nodded coolly and picked up her embroidery again. But only moments later, she whispered, "Why would you ask such a thing?"

"I shouldn't say, milady."

"Oh, nonsense," Caroline said. "I felt I had to scold you just now, but of course I did not mean it. Tell me why you made that remark."

"Pardon me, milady, but I have eyes."

"And..."

"And I've seen the way you two look at each other. You're always making excuses to go to the stables and visit your favorite mare. But when you get there, you spend all your time talking to Michael, smiling up at him, touching his hand. I've seen that, too."

Caroline blushed hotly. "You see too much, Olivia."

"Perhaps. But if I may say so, Michael is twice the man your cousin Viscount Tancred is. Oh, all this class division is ridiculous." She tossed aside the skein of thread she'd begun to unravel for Caroline's embroidery, thinking not only of her mistress and Michael but of herself and Gabriel. "If I may say so," she added quickly.

"You may. And I know what you mean about my *distant* cousin, Jeremy. But all noblemen are not like him. And I must marry from the peerage. That is the way things are, Olivia. We cannot change society."

Liv bit back her response. It was fruitless to argue with Caroline, who was a woman of her times, just as Liv was a woman of hers. "What other gossip did you hear?" she asked, changing the subject.

Caroline lowered her voice and leaned close to Liv. "The Highwayman has ridden again!"

"The Highwayman?" Liv managed to squeak, a chill traveling along her skin.

"Yes, and he was quite daring this time," Caroline confided. "He robbed a carriage that was leaving the sheriff's estate. Can you imagine such arrogance? Sheriff Fremont is in a terrible fury, they say."

"I should think so," Liv responded, trying to contain her mounting anger at Gabriel. How could he be so damned foolish and put himself in such danger? "When did this happen?" Liv asked warily.

"Just a day or two ago, I believe."

Liv's lips shut in a tight line as she remembered waking up two days ago, just before dawn, in an empty bed. At sunrise, Gabriel had slipped in beside her, saying that he'd been in the barn, helping Michael tend a sick horse. She'd believed him because she'd wanted to.

"There's even worse news," Caroline told her. "I probably wasn't supposed to know, but I overheard the servants talking. Another girl has been killed. Strangled."

Liv felt sick. "That same night?" she blurted out.

"No, it's doubtful. At least, no one can say how long her body had lain upon the moor."

Even so, Liv couldn't help her irritation with Gabriel. He'd put himself in a dangerous position by riding around the parish like an avenging fury. Of course, he was the Highwayman, but in that role, he left himself open for all kinds of other accusations.

"You shouldn't talk of such horrors," she said to Caroline, all the while trying to think of an excuse to get back to the house, to find Gabriel and learn what the hell was happening.

"Gabriel would be angry if he knew I listened to gossip. He has always been very strict about that." Caroline dimpled prettily. "But he does not know everything, does he?"

"No, he doesn't, but neither do we, and we haven't planned well today." The excuse came to her quickly. "We've come out with no parasol to protect you from the sun."

"But there is shade here, Olivia—"

"Not enough for your fair complexion."

Before Caroline could respond, Liv was running across the lawn of Northcliffe Manor, heading into the house.

She flew down the hall and opened the library door without knocking. Gabriel stood in front of the mantel, a large book in his hand. She barreled in, slamming the door behind her.

"Are you mad?" she cried.

"Olivia—"

"I don't know who is crazier, you or that dotty old King George..."

Gabriel threw back his head and laughed.

"This isn't funny." She charged toward him.

He caught her in his arms, still laughing. "Olivia, you are a very amusing woman, but why must you always burst in with accusations?"

"I don't always 'burst in.' I've only done it twice, and both times I had a good reason."

"All right," he said. "Let's hear this one. But first..." He leaned over and kissed her.

It was a very thorough kiss. For a moment, she forgot why she was there. His kiss filled her with longing and brought back memories of their lovemaking, which always began with such a kiss. She gave herself to the warmth of his lips and tongue and the total taste of him. He cupped her face in his strong hands and continued to kiss her lingeringly as if he had all the time in the world.

But Liv couldn't get rid of the terrible premonition that time was running out—for both of them. She pulled away.

"All right, tell me," he advised.

"The Highwayman is riding again. *You're* riding again. And this time you went too far, Gabriel, robbing the sheriff's guests!"

He held her at arm's length. "Who has been gossiping to you?"

"One of the maids," she lied, to protect Caroline. "You're going to be caught, Gabe. I read about it in—"

"Yes, I know, your book. That damnable, absurd book which you keep harping on tells you that I am to be captured. I find that interesting, Olivia. Especially since you have no evidence that I am the Highwayman. Only your vivid imagination."

"I didn't imagine that you left our bed in the middle of the night, not to tend your horse but to ride him—right up to the sheriff's manor house, of all places. That's very dangerous, Gabe, especially since another woman has been murdered—"

He dropped his hands from her shoulders, and his face paled. "I had not heard of the murder."

Because he seemed so truly shaken, Liv was moved to slip her arm around his waist. "You'll be blamed for that, too, if this doesn't stop, Gabriel. It's far too dangerous and it's not a game anymore."

"It was never a game with me." A hard look came into his eyes. "And you know nothing of what is going on, Olivia. You have only suppositions and suspicions."

"Look who's talking."

"'Look who's talking?' What does that mean?"

"It's just another expression from the twentieth century. And it means that you also have only suppositions and suspicions that *I'm* a spy."

"Perhaps we are both wrong. Only time will tell."

"Time is running out, Gabe, and when it does, you'll be dead!"

He smiled and stroked her hair. "That would upset you."

"Of course, you fool. I don't want to lose the man I—"

"Yes, Olivia?"

"I'm very fond of you." She settled for less of an admission than had almost escaped her lips.

He kissed her softly. "And I of you. If there were time, I would show you just how much—here and now on the rug before the fireplace. But alas, I must be off."

"Just a moment longer, Gabe."

He stopped and looked at her with a raised eyebrow.

"For us to talk about this highwayman thing," she added quickly.

"There's nothing further to be said about that, Olivia. And no more gossiping with my sister," he admonished. "I shall be back by nightfall."

He shut the door firmly behind him.

"Damn," Olivia fumed. He refused to hear her warnings. And if she didn't do something soon, he would be arrested and hanged! Unable to bear that thought, she sank onto his desk chair. She'd been at Northcliffe Manor just over a week and in that time had fallen madly in love with a man who lived in another century, a man who was fated to hang.

"Double damn," she cursed again, this time at herself—for loving him. It was true. She was wildly, desperately in love and probably had been from the first time he'd kissed her. Maybe from the first time she'd seen him astride that black stallion. Or even before, when she'd first seen his picture in the book.

It was absurd but very real. Gabriel was the man in *Rogues Across Time*. And Gabriel was going to die. She was overcome by a sense of despair. What could she—a 1990s woman living in a 1790s world—do to save him?

She could change history!

Was that possible? Of course it was. For someone who had just recently traveled backward in time, anything was possible. She had to find a way to keep him from riding again as the Highwayman. But how?

Her head pounding, Liv hurried to Caroline's room and quickly found a parasol. On the wall next to the armoire were miniature paintings of Caroline and Gabriel when they were children. She'd seen them before but this time she noticed Gabriel's protective arm around his sister. He took care of her, then as now, risking everything for the damned Stratton jewels. So Caroline could have a dowry. So he could avenge his family's honor.

He must have accumulated enough money by now, riding as the Highwayman, to do the necessary repairs to Northcliffe Manor and add some horses to his stables. The damned Stratton jewels were the problem— and Gabe's sense of family honor. Her earlier hunch had obviously been right. He didn't know which of the parish's devious noblemen had the jewels, but if someone could find out . . .

Once the jewels were returned to Northcliffe Manor, surely Gabe would willingly give up his dangerous alter ego—the Highwayman.

With that deduction lingering in her mind, Liv realized that she'd spent too long with her thoughts and hurried back to the garden, clutching the parasol.

Caroline looked up from her embroidery. "You were gone a very long time," she chided. "Did you see my brother?"

"No. Uh, well, yes. Just for a moment." Liv lowered her eyes guiltily, wondering how much Caroline suspected about her and Gabriel.

"Something must have upset him. He stormed through the garden and thundered away on Eclipse, his favorite stallion."

Liv's mind worked frantically, her thoughts flying in different directions. Had she upset him with mention of the murder? Had he ridden away to follow his suspicions and seek a killer? She wondered how she could take advantage of his absence to do some sleuthing of her own.

"Oh, dear," Caroline said, interrupting her thoughts. "I am out of blue thread."

Liv tried not to react too quickly before suggesting, "I could go to the village for you. Isn't this market day?"

"Yes, would you find the housekeeper and ask her to—"

"She's already left for the village, Lady Caroline. Besides, she wouldn't know the right shade."

"Possibly not." Caroline agreed.

"Let me go for you."

Caroline tilted the parasol. "All right, Olivia. My allowance is in the small purse in my dressing table—"

Before she could finish, Liv was heading back across the lawn, her plan forming rapidly. It would take most of Caroline's coins to carry it out. But she'd explain everything to her mistress later. She couldn't worry about it now.

THE STREETS of Haroldsgate were crowded on market day with carts and stalls from which farmers sold and bartered their goods. The sharp scent of great rounds of cheddar cheese vied with the fragrance of baking pies and helped disguise the odor of unwashed bodies and dirty clothes. The eighteenth century, Liv observed, had a lot to learn about personal hygiene.

She pushed through the crowd, managing to avoid squealing pigs and clucking chickens, not to mention Simon and Nora, of whom she caught a glimpse as they bartered with a farmer at his vegetable bin. She ducked out of sight until they completed their purchases and then slipped between two stalls of bright flowers and saw the woman she'd been searching for.

The Northcliffe Manor housekeeper was busy supervising purchases. Liv tugged at her apron. "Mrs. Thornwhistle, I wonder if you would help me."

The housekeeper turned her considerable girth toward Liv.

"It'll only take a minute. I—I need to talk to the housekeepers from the homes of Lords Cardiff and Livingstone." She decided to start with the most obvious suspects, just as in the mysteries she'd read.

"Go away, wench. I have more to do than traffic with the likes of ye. And why are ye even in town today?"

"Lady Caroline sent me. For—for some thread."

"Then go about yer task and don't bother me."

Liv decided to take a chance. "There is a young man," she said quickly. "He's a footman at one of the great homes, but I'm not quite sure which. I want to send him a note."

The housekeeper frowned, wrinkling her forehead and puffing out her wide pink cheeks. "Ye should be paying attention to your duties, not running about like a lightskirt—"

"Please, Mrs. Thornwhistle. It'll only take a moment, and then I'll get right to my duties. If you'll just send me in the direction of the housekeepers."

"And how d'ye suggest I do that in this crowded market?"

She had a point, Liv thought sadly. It looked like a wild-goose chase. Mrs. Thornwhistle wasn't about to go searching around the market for the other two women.

"Ye be in luck," Mrs. Thornwhistle said suddenly, looking up from the basket of eggs she was collecting. "The two of 'em just went into that far stall, to sample the ale, I be thinking. 'Stead of working," she added with a loud hmmph.

THE HOUSEKEEPERS were an ill-matched pair, one tall and lanky with a large jutting nose and a fierce expression, the other tiny and pink-cheeked with curly white hair escaping from her cap. Liv prayed the kind-looking, grandmotherly one would have the information she needed.

"Ladies," Liv greeted them, remembering her ye's and thee's. "May I buy ye another ale?"

The women regarded her with unconcealed suspicion.

"I be from Northcliffe Manor, and Mrs. Thornwhistle instructed me to treat ye." Liv pointed vaguely to where the housekeeper had been, relieved she was no longer there.

The women looked even more dubious.

"To make amends...for whatever happened among ye." She had no idea that anything *had* happened, but knowing Mrs. Thornwhistle's personality, it was a safe bet.

"'Tis about time," said the tall one, holding out her mug to the wizened little man beside the ale barrel.

Liv smiled and joined them at the makeshift bar.

Soon she was on a first-name basis with the women. Maude, the taller foreboding-looking one, turned out to be a sweetheart, and Ellie, short and plump and prone to spontaneous laughter, was also quick to anger and used the salty language of a sailor. But a few mugs of ale made her less formidable, and Liv finally got up the nerve to turn their conversation to the ladies of the manor houses.

"My mistress Caroline is quite the lady," she began. "Why, her dresses be as elegant as any, sewn with tiny stitches the eye can hardly see." She put down her mug, squelched a burp and decided it was time to stop drinking the heavy brown ale and fake it instead.

Ellie reared back on her heels and regarded Liv with bleary eyes. "'Taint no one can match Lady Cardiff for fineness. Her clothes come direct from Paris."

"So do me lady's, I'm sure," Liv said.

"Ha! Ye got maggots in yer loft if ye think that!"

While Liv was chuckling to herself at the expression, Maude jumped in. "'Taint the dresses so much as the jewels. And ye ain't seen anything like me mistress's jewels."

Liv's heart quickened. It was what she'd been waiting to hear. Cardiff and Livingstone, along with Fremont, the high sheriff, had been gambling buddies of the late baron. There was more than an even chance that the Stratton jewels were hidden away at one of those estates, spoils of a crooked card game.

She tried to keep her voice casual. "Me mistress has a fine set of pearls and garnets." It wasn't a lie. She'd seen the jewelry.

"Pearls, pah." Maude slurred her words. "Lady Livingstone don't care much for those. She has an emerald and diamond necklace neither one of ye have seen the likes of."

But Ellie wasn't to be outdone. Barely able to stand upright at this point, she held on to the bar. "Rubies and sapphires, my Lady Cardiff has. Which of ye can say that?"

Liv was silent, trying not to reveal her growing excitement. Maude made a noise of defeat as Ellie continued triumphantly. "Blue and red, they be. A huge round bib of jewels and earbobs to match."

Liv was giddy with triumph. The Stratton jewels! Of course, the jewels in the tiara had been reset into earrings and the extra stones had been added to make a larger necklace.

"I never heard tell of 'em," Maude said with a tone of jealous defeat.

"'Course ye ain't. She don't wear 'em 'round these parts. Society here ain't fine enough for her. Keeps 'em in a safe, she does."

And Liv knew why. She didn't want to display them for the Highwayman! "Too bad," she said, realizing that safe breaking at the Cardiff estate was beyond her capabilities. "It seems a shame not to show 'em off."

"Aye, but that proves what ye know. In two days she be takin' 'em to London to wear at court," Ellie bragged. "She's 'ad the maids sewin' and pressin' her clothes for weeks. Ye'd think she were goin' to meet the bloody king."

"Mad as 'e is, 'e might not notice if she were stark naked," Maude commented.

Liv's heart was beating so loudly she could hardly hear their comments. "To London . . . Is it a long trip?"

"Are ye daft? 'Course it is. She'll 'ave us scurryin' around at daybreak so's she can be gone by high noon."

"I guess there be only one road to London." Liv's voice trembled with excitement.

Lor', yes," Maude exclaimed. "Ye're not from these parts, are ye?"

"No, I'm not. I don't even know yer lady's carriage."

"Everyone else does! All white and gilt with the family crest painted on the door."

Liv desperately tried to hide her smile of satisfaction by involving herself with the tab. She kept one coin and gave the rest of the money in her pocket to the ale man. "I have to take my leave now, to do some shopping for my lady."

Both women looked disappointed, but Liv slipped away and quickly lost herself in the crowd. She had the information she needed, but did she have the resolve to do what had to be done next?

LIV TRUDGED along the road toward Northcliffe Manor thinking of how she'd always struggled to do the right thing in her life. Now here she was, in another time, contemplating larcenous deeds. So far, she'd lied, stolen and bribed. Could she take the next step?

She saw him then, cutting across the field toward her. Her heart leaped in anticipation, as always. Now the excitement was coupled with nervousness. It seemed as if she'd been telling lies all day, and she wondered if she could keep her stories straight with Gabe.

She ran down the hill to meet him. "Gabe, I didn't know you'd be back so soon."

"Nor did I know you would be gone so long," he replied.

She wondered if they were playing a game of cat and mouse. Could he have thought she was spying on him and, turning the tables, spied on *her*? Damn! This could get complicated.

"The time got away from me. You know how it is when a woman goes shopping," she responded quickly, and then tried to turn the game around again. "Did you have a nice time this afternoon?"

His face tightened. "My trip was not for pleasure." He wrapped his arm around her. "But I assume yours was. Tell me all about Haroldsgate."

He won that round, Liv thought as she let herself fit comfortably into his clasp and walked along beside him. She could tell about the market without mentioning the housekeepers, but she'd have to be careful. There were pitfalls everywhere.

"I've never seen quite so many pigs in the same place at one time," she said in an attempt to describe her day.

He laughed along with her, but he could tell that her remark came from nerves. She couldn't meet his eyes directly, and her voice sounded high and anxious. He wondered what she'd been up to, this brazen woman who was almost fearless in her trickery.

She fascinated him and, spy or not, he still desired her with a white-hot need that grew with each passing hour. He'd thought about their kiss all day. It was an opportunity missed because he'd had to leave on what turned out to be a fool's mission. The man he'd gone looking for was nowhere to be found. The jackal had gone to ground.

He pulled her closer, his fingers grasping the cool smooth skin of her upper arm. She gave him a sideways glance under lowered lashes. The look was innocent, he thought, but also coquettish and alluring.

"I know what you were doing this afternoon." He made the statement idly, almost casually, and noted that she missed a step.

"What—"

"A meeting with your spymasters, I think."

She let out a long breath, and to his surprise, she giggled.

"It must have been hard for you to have to admit that you had learned nothing more about the Highwayman."

"Not difficult at all," she said. I didn't tell anybody anything because I'm *not* a spy."

He smiled to himself.

"But I did something foolish, Gabe." She stopped and gazed up at him. "And I hope you'll help me." She tilted her head back to get a look at his face, which was still slightly suspicious but interested. Crossing her fingers, she lied again.

"I got involved in a game of chance at the market and lost all my money."

He smiled. "My fair Olivia a gambler?"

"Not usually, but it was so tempting, I couldn't resist. So I need . . . That is, if I could just have an advance on my salary . . ." She cocked her head. "I do get a salary, don't I?"

"Wages? Yes, of course, but only quarterly, paid out by the butler. But if it is money you need, you have only to ask me. How much did you lose?"

She looked sheepish. "A shilling, sixpence."

"You shall have it."

She let out a long sigh, hoping this would be the end of further talk about market day and her agenda. "I'll pay you back. It's only a loan," she advised with a stubborn lift of her chin.

"I understand that you will not be my kept woman, as you have so often told me." He kissed her forehead. "I never think of you that way, only as my fascinating, mysterious and always surprising lover." He leaned closer, his lips searching for hers.

As she raised her face toward him, a fleeting movement caught her eye, and she turned toward it. "Gabe, look—the deer."

He followed her gaze. Moving from the shadow of a copse of trees into the twilight of a meadow were a stag, three does and two fawns. "The Northcliffe deer. They have been on this land for as many generations as my own family," he said proudly.

"So beautiful . . . Do you hunt them?" she asked tentatively, well aware that hunting was a way of life here.

"No. My ancestors did a good job of almost eliminating them so I have allowed the herds to build up. They are like a talisman, wild and free, beautiful and gentle." He seemed to redden slightly as he added, "Sometimes I feed them, in the depths of winter when the snow is too heavy for them to forage."

Liv felt her heart skip a beat. "You feed them?"

He shrugged and looked back toward the deer. "Foolish, I know, but I want them to stay here on this land, forever."

She felt the hot sting of tears in her eyes. Spontaneously throwing her arms around his neck, she said, "You're just like my grandfather."

Gabe laughed. "I sincerely hope not."

"Only in your kindness and gentleness. Grandfather fed the deer on his farm, too. For the same reasons." She stood on tiptoe and kissed him. "Despite the fact that you're stubborn and foolish, you're the most wonderful man, Gabriel. I'm so glad I found you."

He grinned sardonically. "I believe I found *you*, Olivia."

"Then I came all this way, backward in time, just so you *could* find me, and I'm glad. Because we're together." At least for this moment, she thought, holding on to him tightly. Now, more than ever, Liv knew she had to save him, no matter what it took.

As they stood together on the hillside watching the deer, she knew that she loved this complex man, who was headstrong and powerful, gentle and caring, loyal and protective of those he loved. A man for his century—or any century.

7

"I'D GIVE a year's salary for a safety pin," Liv muttered as she struggled with the buttons on the riding habit she'd borrowed from Caroline. "If I knew what my salary was."

Not only was the riding skirt half a foot too short, it didn't begin to make it all the way around her middle. She pulled at the waistband, trying at least to close the gap, but it wasn't possible. A wide expanse of skin remained uncovered.

Frowning, she examined herself in the pedestal mirror, not surprised to find that she looked ridiculous. First, there was the skirt, a full inch short of closure even when she sucked in her breath. Then, the jacket didn't even meet across her breasts. She could solve that by leaving it open over her blouse, and if she wore her boots, the length of the skirt wouldn't be too noticeable. But without a safety pin, she'd never be able to keep the skirt up, much less fastened.

She simply wasn't believable, not in the role she'd chosen for herself—a gentlewoman dressed in the latest chic riding habit, off for a late-morning canter. Blast her last minute bad luck.

Up until now, everything had fallen into place. Gabriel had gone off for the day on one of his mysterious errands, and Caroline had been invited for a two-day house party some twenty miles away. Of course, she'd wanted her lady's maid to accompany her, but Liv had feigned illness—and been believed.

It was an acting performance that, in her opinion, was worthy of an Academy Award. She had everyone, even Gabe, believing that she was ill with pleurisy. She'd never been quite sure what that was, but she moaned mightily, complained first of stomach pains, and then a headache, and finally chest congestion. That one seemed to cause the most concern so she decided it was a pleurisy symptom and coughed appropriately.

With the greatest sympathy, Caroline had agreed to be accompanied by one of the housemaids and, after seeing Liv settled comfortably in bed, suggested various cures.

"Many people recommend rattlesnake root," she told Liv.

"How about hot tea or broth?" Liv suggested.

"Not as effective, I shouldn't think."

"Could I try them first?" Liv asked—and breathed with relief when Caroline ordered the cook to prepare them for her.

As soon as Caroline left, she put her plan into action. Now all she needed was a few more hours of good fortune to carry it out. Except she couldn't get the damned skirt buttoned. Frustrated, she searched through the drawers of Caroline's bureau for some kind of sash.

It was strange, she mused, pushing aside a pile of embroidered handkerchiefs, what she did and didn't miss from the twentieth century. Safety pins were more important than the obvious things. Like television and telephones, newspapers and magazines or even modern transportation. She didn't have a car in the city, and buses and subways weren't the kinds of things a person would go back to the twentieth century for. No, horses were just fine. Or so she thought; she'd find out soon.

"This will do it." In the back of a drawer, she found a wide striped scarf and tied it around her waist, holding up the skirt and concealing the gap. She looped another silk scarf around her neck. It would come in handy later.

How the hell she was going to explain all this to Caroline, Liv had no idea. She'd worry about that later.

The hairdo was next. No eighteenth-century lady would wear her hair flowing loose over her shoulders. "Rubber bands" she murmured. "I miss rubber bands and mousse, too." With a sigh of resignation, she pulled her hair back into a loose chignon at the base of her neck, securing it with hairpins. At least *they'd* been invented by now. But they didn't totally do the trick. Uncontrollable curly pieces stuck out around her face, and no matter how hard she pulled them back and pinned them down, the tendrils seemed to have a will of their own.

"Yep, I definitely miss hair mousse," she announced to her image in the mirror. "And hot and cold running water. And toothpaste." She'd been amazed to learn that factory-made toothbrushes were available, but teeth were simply "washed," with nothing that could begin to duplicate her familiar toothpaste.

"And tissues," she added. It was a pain always carrying a fresh handkerchief. But she tucked one of Caroline's lace hankies in her sleeve because a lady wouldn't leave the house without one. Or a hat. Caroline's were neatly arranged in boxes on top of the armoire. Liv pulled out a silly felt one replete with feathers. It would complete her outfit perfectly and maybe take attention away from her ill-fitting riding habit. She secured it to her hair with a wicked-looking hat pin.

Surveying herself once more in the mirror, she groaned audibly. If she was a lady, she was an absurd-looking one. She shrugged. This was the best she could do. Crossing her fingers, she headed for the stables and prayed her luck would continue.

MICHAEL GAVE HER a very strange look, which she expected had to do with her bizarre outfit.

"I thought you were too ill to leave your room, Olivia." Arms folded grandly across his broad chest, he observed her with suspicion.

"I was, but I recovered," she replied with a bright smile.

"I recollect hearing Lady Caroline say that 'twould be a day or two before you were up and about," he continued, apparently far from convinced.

"I know, it was really a miraculous recovery, Michael. Do you know, I think it was because of Cook's recipes."

"Rattlesnake root, I believe."

"No! Lady Caroline had Cook prepare broth and tea."

"Yes, rattlesnake-root broth. 'Deed, it must be what cured you."

Even though she hadn't been sick in the first place, she'd drunk the herbal tea—and eaten the soup. "Ugh," she said, thinking of what she'd gone through in order to carry out her plan.

"And I'm heartily pleased to see your swift recovery."

"Yes." She gulped. "I'm quite well now. I hope. And I'm ready for a ride. The baron told you that I'm allowed to go riding, didn't he?"

"'Deed so, Olivia. I also recollect that you were to have lessons first."

"They're not necessary, really, as long as you choose a gentle mount for me."

"To be sure, I'll do just that." Michael looked her up and down, a smile tugging at his lips. "Looks like you're wearing one of Lady Caroline's cast-off riding habits."

Liv tugged at the short jacket. "Well, yes. Lady Caroline is very generous." Sharing that assumption with Michael was another thing she would have to admit to her mistress later, Liv thought with a sigh.

Michael's smile widened. "She is more than generous. She's perfect, isn't she? Once a bonnie lass, she has grown into a great lady—"

"Who wishes she could be a farmer's wife someday," Liv interrupted.

Michael looked down, blushing. "Would that such a thing were possible." Then he quickly recovered and began sputtering denials.

"I know she slips away to meet you, Michael. Who do you think covers for her?"

He looked up with surprise. "You don't suppose his lordship knows, do you?"

Liv shook her head. "Nope, and I'm not telling. The baron has more than enough on his mind, as it is."

"I'm heartily grateful to you."

Liv patted his arm assuredly. "Now it's time for me to get going."

"Off to someplace special, are you?" he asked with polite curiosity.

"No, no," she lied, fighting to keep her voice casual and thinking how much both of them were hiding from Gabe. She wondered if there was such an expression as "cover-up" in this century. "I'm just out for a ride. Maybe toward the London Road. Is it difficult to find?"

"Easy," came the laconic response. "'Tis the only road in the parish." He studied her speculatively, and this time Liv was the one to lower her eyes.

"I'll get the groom to saddle up our gentlest mare, old Gracie." He shot her a devilish grin. "Sure you know how to ride, are you, Olivia?"

"Of course," she responded. She hadn't been on a horse in years, except behind Gabe, and could only hope it was something that came back, like riding a bicycle. Whatever happened once she was in the saddle, she couldn't turn back. It was now or never.

She paced nervously up and down until the groom led out a plump brown mare. That's when she saw the sidesaddle. Damn. She almost cursed aloud but managed to restrain herself. Of course, in this era, women didn't straddle a horse like men, which was why she was wearing a riding habit with a skirt rather than pants. She just hadn't thought about it.

"Is something the matter, Olivia?" Michael asked.

"Of course not." Olivia walked to the mounting box and stepped onto it confidently, wondering what the hell to do next and what leg went where. While Michael and the groom waited beside Gracie, Liv managed to figure it out and placed her left foot in the stirrup. Then she settled into the saddle, hooked her right leg over the saddle horn and smiled down at them victoriously.

Michael grasped the lead line and headed out of the stable with Liv frantically trying to get into the rhythm of the horse's movement and just as frantically trying not to let the men see how awkward she felt. Her position was uncomfortable, and her balance was precarious. She could feel the silly hat tipping down over her forehead, but she was too nervous to take her hands off the reins to straighten it.

As they reached the manor driveway, Michael unhooked the line and Liv was on her own. Trying to look in control, she jiggled the reins and was gratified when the horse moved into a walk only slightly faster than the one that had gotten them this far.

"We'll be fine," she said, as much to convince herself as the men.

Michael's voice floated lazily on the breeze. She probably wasn't meant to hear, but she did.

"'Oh, wad some power, the giftie gae us, to see ourselves as ithers see us.'"

Liv recognized the line from a Robert Burns poem. So Michael had been quoting the Scottish poet, not creating on the spot, the night of the ball! The men's low laughter followed her, but rather than feel embarrassed, Liv was impressed by the steward's knowledge.

She smiled back at him and then, holding her head high, rode grandly down the driveway, determined not to fall off.

GETTING OFF the horse nearly an hour later was much more difficult than mounting had been, but she managed to execute the task without letting go of the reins and losing old Gracie.

After tying her reluctant mount to a large branch in a shelter of trees, she sat down to wait at the side of the London Road, halfway, she had judged, between Northcliffe Manor and the Cardiff estate. She knew there were hundreds of things that could go wrong with her plan. Starting with the timing. What if she'd already missed Lady Cardiff? Or, if and when the carriage showed up, what if she didn't have the courage to execute her plan?

She tugged at her skirt to get more comfortable and leaned back against the hillside, thinking about what she was up to. The thought caused a sharp twinge of conscience. Her grandmother had constantly lectured that the ends never justified the means, but in this case, Liv felt there was no choice. She had to do something to get Gabriel's attention, something outrageous, and certainly nothing was more outrageous than her plan.

Liv wondered what kind of odds a Las Vegas bookie would give her for carrying it out. She laughed to herself. Ten to one against? No, probably more like a hundred to one! She was determined to beat the odds. Which was going to require more than just a positive attitude. Unfortunately, that was all she had.

Liv sat back, chewing on a blade of grass, and began to give herself a pep talk about the rightness of her plan. She was at a high point on the road. It was a clear day, and she had a view of several miles. She would have plenty of time to prepare. Her clothes, as uncomfortable as they were, looked convincing, at least from far away. Best of all, what she had in her pocket would change the odds dramatically in her favor.

She was still mentally listing the pluses, when she saw a puff of dust in the distance. She bolted upright, shading her eyes and watching as the dot grew larger and larger until it became recognizable. She moved to the edge of the road but didn't take her eyes off the carriage, white with gilt trimmings and bearing the family coat of arms on the door. Just as described by the housekeeper, it was the Cardiff coach!

Liv pulled up the white scarf she'd wrapped around her neck and quickly covered her nose and mouth. She wasn't the Lone Ranger, but her disguise would have to do, she thought, as she settled herself in the middle of the road, stretched out with her face down—almost. She turned enough to watch the carriage approach. Coming up the incline, the driver would have plenty of time to see her and stop. She hoped. Being trampled by a carriage and four horses was definitely *not* part of her plan.

The horses galloped toward her; she could feel the reverberation of their hoofbeats in the earth. As she watched the carriage approach, she saw not only the driver atop his perch, but another man beside him, holding what looked like a gun. "Damn," she swore into her mask. Of course, there would be a guard. The

Highwayman was at large. It was all Gabe's fault. Well, she'd just have to worry about the second man when the carriage stopped—if it ever did.

It kept on coming. How long did it take a carriage to stop? she wondered, and suddenly realized that she'd lost her cool. Her heart was pounding furiously. Then—finally—she heard the driver's cry. He saw her and stood up, pulling back on the reins.

"Whoa! Whoa, horses."

They slowed to a trot but didn't stop. Liv felt the blood rushing wildly in her ears. She could hear the rattle of harnesses and the pounding of hooves. She could even hear the horses' breathing as they got closer and closer.

Then they stopped, just a few yards away. Liv's heart was beating faster than she imagined possible. God, what had she gotten herself into?

Another voice called out, querulous and demanding, "Shelton, why have you stopped the carriage? We are behind schedule now."

"Sorry, your ladyship, but someone appears to have fallen in the road. A lady, by the looks of her."

The woman's voice sounded resigned. "Then see to her. But hurry."

"Stay," the guard ordered the driver. "I'll take care of the lady."

Liv peeked quickly and saw that the man *did* have a gun. This definitely wasn't part of her plan, but weapon to weapon, Liv decided she had the advantage. She tensed and held her breath as the man approached.

She turned her head away, out of his view, as the steps came closer, crunching on the rocks beside her.

Her hand was in her pocket, clutching her weapon, ready. She felt his touch on her shoulder.

"Madam, are you—"

She rolled over, the container of pepper spray in her hand, directed at the guard. One squirt into his face, and the man was her victim.

Liv watched as he screamed and grabbed his eyes, staggering backward. She stood up, holding the pepper spray like a weapon, ready to use it again. But he'd dropped the gun and, still screaming, headed into the woods. For a split second, Liv watched him and was momentarily contrite. She looked at the can. Could this stuff blind you? No, she'd been assured when she bought it in New York, the loss of vision was only temporary. And in a matter of minutes, the guard would realize that and be back.

Quickly, she picked up his gun and ran toward the carriage. The driver hadn't moved except to raise his hands over his head.

"Just stay like that and I'll let you live, Shelton," she said as she flung open the carriage door. Two women, their eyes wide with fright, were huddled in the corner. Unsure of what they had witnessed, she decided they would probably be more intimidated by the gun than the pepper spray. Liv pocketed the spray and hoisted the musket to her shoulder. It was heavier than it looked, but she managed to point it in the general direction of the women.

One was a plump plain woman in gray. Definitely not the grand lady. *She* was finely dressed, with a large hat above small hard eyes.

"Stand and deliver, Lady Cardiff," Liv bellowed in her best Highwayman imitation. "Hand over your jewel box now or death will be your fate."

The women screamed in unison, but it was Lady Cardiff who promptly fainted.

Liv realized that her hands were shaking, and she tried to steady the gun and point it at the woman in gray. "All right, you, give me the jewel box," Liv said as she shoved the gun closer, almost in the woman's nose. "And be quick about it." The terrified woman quickly reached under the seat and pulled out an ornately carved wooden box, which she held toward Liv.

Liv leaned the gun against the carriage and grabbed the box. She started to lift the lid and realized it was locked.

"The key, the key!" she demanded.

Pale with fear, the woman answered in a voice that was no more than a whisper. "My mistress has hidden it. I don't know where."

Liv reached over and shook Lady Cardiff roughly by the shoulders. Her head bobbed back and forth but she remained unconscious.

There was no way Liv would be able to get on the horse with the heavy box. And she only wanted the Northcliffe jewels, not the whole collection. She backed away, holding the box, and glanced up at Shelton. He hadn't moved a millimeter. But she heard something in the woods, a voice calling out.

Perspiration broke out on her forehead. Liv knew she would never shoot the guard, even if she knew how. She had a feeling it wasn't just a matter of pulling the trigger. And if he got the gun away from her, she wouldn't have a chance to use the spray again.

Taking a deep breath, she lifted the box above her head and threw it with all her might against the rocks at the side of the road. It split open, and the jewelry spilled out, diamonds, pearls, emeralds, multicolored tiaras, bracelets and rings. And there, glittering more brightly than any of them, the sparkling sapphires and rubies set into earrings and a wide necklace. Liv grabbed them and stuffed them into her pockets.

Looking back, she saw the maid vainly trying to rouse Lady Cardiff with smelling salts. Above them, on his perch, Shelton still sat with his hands in the air.

"Good man, Shelton," she said. "Just stay like that until I'm gone." Liv grabbed the gun and ran toward the trees where her horse waited. She'd done it! She'd retrieved the Stratton jewels. Now all she had to do was make her escape.

As she reached the horse, she turned to see the guard break through the trees on the other side of the road, heading toward her.

"Now, Gracie, if you've ever obeyed commands in your life, do it now." She flung the reins over Gracie's head and ran around to the hillside to mount. "Stay," she said. "I mean, steady." "Stay" was for dogs, she realized. From her position on the hill, she easily reached over, slipping her foot into the stirrup.

"Steady, now. Don't budge." Still holding the unwieldy gun, she grasped the saddle horn with her free hand and settled onto her mount only seconds before the guard started up the hill toward her.

Liv hooked her knee over the saddle horn, leaned forward and kicked Gracie's flanks with all her might.

To her surprise, the horse sprang into action and took off through the woods with a burst of speed that rocked her in the saddle.

Her hat flew off, and the scarf slipped from her face, caught in the wind and blew away. She wrapped the reins over the saddle horn, clutched a handful of mane and let the horse run. But there was no way she could hold on to both Gracie's neck *and* the gun and still stay on the damned horse. As they broke out of the woods and crossed a meadow of fresh spring grass, she flung the weapon away—and scared the daylights out of her horse.

Fat old Gracie, traveling at what Liv thought was her top speed, took the bit in her mouth and raced flat out with the velocity of a derby contender. Liv was flung sideways, bouncing erratically, and nearly falling from the saddle. With sweating hands, she clung to the horn and managed to right herself. But she wasn't going to be able to hold on much longer.

"Slow down, Gracie," she begged. "Please, slow down!" She pulled on the reins, but it was useless.

Then she heard the hoofbeats behind her. Another horse and rider, racing, catching up. Could it be the guard—or the sheriff, coming after her so soon? She wanted to turn and look but feared the movement would knock her off and send her under Gracie's hooves.

She fought down a rush of blind panic and tried to lean low over the horse's neck as she'd seen cowboys do in westerns. But cowboys obviously didn't ride sidesaddle! Her balance was too precarious with her leg hooked over the saddle horn. She couldn't hang on much longer. She was going to fall!

The hoofbeats from behind grew closer and louder until the horse and rider were beside her. From the corner of her eye, Liv saw the head and neck of a great black stallion. A man's arm reached out, grabbed her around the waist and lifted her from the saddle.

For a long moment, Liv was suspended in the air, her legs moving rapidly, like the legs of a swimmer trying to keep afloat. Then, suddenly, her body crashed against the rider. She flung her arms around him and held on for dear life. He slowed his horse from a gallop to a trot and then a walk, while, far ahead, Gracie continued her wild run.

When they stopped, Liv slid to the ground and looked up at him. "Gabe, my wonderful savior, to the rescue again!" Gabriel dismounted and she flung her arms around his neck, kissing him repeatedly. "You're my hero," she told him.

"My horse and I," he corrected. "You owe much to Eclipse."

Liv patted the horse on the neck and quipped, "Thanks, worthy steed."

"Very lucky for you that Eclipse and I were in this meadow when old Gracie raced through. She was headed for the barn as if the hounds of hell were after her." He stopped, frowning. "Now, tell me what is going on, Olivia—" he gave her a long look from head to toe "—and why you are wearing that costume."

Liv avoided his gaze, contemplating the best way to tell him what she'd done. Letting out a huge sigh, she opted for the truth, which she blurted it out in one quick sentence. "I just held up Lady Cardiff's carriage and stole back the Stratton jewels."

Gabriel stared in disbelief. "I assume this is another facet of your colorful imagination, just like those stories of being transported from the future."

"Both are true," Liv said. "But I can prove only this one." She reached into her pocket and pulled out the necklace and earrings. "Hold out your hands."

Looking more puzzled than ever, he did what she asked, and she dropped the jewels onto his upturned palms. They glittered brilliantly in the sunlight.

Gabriel felt his heart miss a beat as he held the jewelry almost reverently. "These are beautiful but," he stammered, "they are not the Stratton jewels." Even as he spoke the words, he wasn't sure of their truth. "Our jewels were set into a tiara and a smaller necklace."

"Of course, and they've been reset so they won't be recognized. Not by the average person, anyway. But I'm not a novice, Gabriel. I can see what they've done. Look here—" she indicated a link in the necklace "—and here around this stone. These are the reset Stratton jewels, won—or stolen—from your father by Lord Cardiff in a card game. Cardiff was one of the gamblers, wasn't he?"

"He was one of them, yes, but—"

"He was *the* one who stole the jewels and gave them to his wife," she said definitely.

"We cannot be sure of that." But Gabriel knew she was right. He was holding in his hands the Stratton jewels. No other rubies and sapphires in the land were cut so perfectly or gleamed with such magnificence. "I am not certain I want to hear this, but it is probably time for you to tell me how you managed to steal them."

"To steal what, Gabriel?"

He smiled down at her. "The Stratton jewels. You are right, Olivia. These are our family jewels, Caroline's dowry. Now, I want the truth about how you acquired them." He was unwilling to believe that the slender woman beside him had, in the past hour, perpetrated highway robbery on one of the foremost families in the parish.

"First, I had to locate the jewels, which I did after buying a couple of rounds of ale for the house servants—"

"The servants?"

"Something a baron wouldn't think of. Though I must admit that I used Caroline's money—which you later reimbursed," she added. "It was a good investment. I learned that no one outside the household knew who had the jewels. Lord and Lady Cardiff were very slick."

"Then what, Olivia?" His voice held an incredulous edge.

"I pretended I was hurt. I lay down in the road, and when Lady Cardiff's carriage stopped, I subdued the guard—"

"There was a guard?"

"Yes, I expect you were the reason for that, frightening all those people when you rode as the Highwayman. But don't worry, I subdued him with my pepper spray—"

"What is this pepper spray?"

She showed him the container that she'd brought from the twentieth century. He studied it carefully. "This is like nothing I have ever seen. I assume it somehow propels red pepper into your victim's face."

"Something like that. The guard wasn't blinded permanently, only temporarily. I took his gun—"

"Good Lord. I do not believe this. How could you have managed such a feat?"

She smiled proudly up at him, and Gabriel was further amazed by his surprising highwaywoman.

"It was easy. He ran off into the woods, so I picked up the gun he'd dropped and turned it on the driver, who already had his hands held above his head. Then I got the jewel box from Lady Cardiff and her maid. Also pretty easy, considering one of them fainted and the other one became hysterical. 'Course, by the time I broke open the chest and reached Gracie, the guard was after me again so we had to hurry."

By now, Gabriel was beyond surprise, his patience evaporating. "Do you realize how dangerous this escapade was? I never would have allowed you to attempt such a thing."

"That's exactly why I didn't tell you! Don't be angry, Gabe."

Her blue eyes were so beseeching that he felt his exasperation fade. "What am I going to do with you, Olivia?"

She put her arms around his waist. "I can think of a lot of things. Be happy we have the jewels, enjoy the day, have a good dinner, make love . . ."

"This is not a game," he said seriously as he reached for Eclipse's reins.

He was still mentally struggling with her story as they began to walk slowly across the meadow with the horse following. "Why, Olivia? Why would you take such a foolish risk?"

"I'll tell you why. If those paste jewels had been Lady Caroline's dowry, eventually someone would have realized they were fake. That's the reason I stole back the real ones. For Caroline—and for you. I wanted to do something drastic that would make you come to your senses about this stupid highwayman role. If the jewels were returned, there would be no reason for you to ride as the Highwayman."

"I've never admitted—"

"Oh, cut it out, Gabe."

He stopped and looked down at her. "'Cut it out'?"

"It means no more lying. *You* know that *I* know you're the Highwayman. If you don't stop, you'll be caught. And if that happens, you'll be hanged. I would have done anything to stop that. Anything!"

Her face and voice reflected the intensity of her feelings, and Gabriel felt his own emotions twist inside him. With her wild stories and boundless passions, Olivia moved him like no other woman. She had risked certain prison and possible death to help him. She had set her own test of loyalty—and passed it with glory and without fear.

Gabriel dropped the reins and took her in his arms. "Forgive me for being exasperated with you. That was only because you were so reckless and foolish—"

"Now you know how I feel," she muttered, "when you go racing about the countryside."

"No one in my life has shown such devotion. I was wrong in thinking that you were a spy." He gazed down at her. "And I rarely admit that I am wrong."

"Thank you, Gabe." She touched his face with her fingertips. "Now that you know I'm not a spy, maybe you'll believe the rest of my story. That I'm from the future."

"Olivia—"

"No, Gabe, listen to me. This is the truth. I'm from the twentieth century, and now I know why I've been sent back in time. I'm here to warn you, to save you, Gabe," she said urgently.

How could he believe such an implausible tale? He knew she wasn't a spy; she'd convinced him of that. But this other story was too preposterous. Was it possible that Olivia, a serving girl from another parish, truly believed that she came from another century? He couldn't prevent a frown from crossing his face.

"No matter the century," he said, "why would you put your life in danger to save me?"

She drew his lips to hers and kissed him with all the sweetness she felt. "Because, Baron Northcliffe, Gabriel Stratton, my own Sir Gabe, I am madly, totally in love with you—and will be forever, in this century or another."

She thought she felt his body tense against hers. "Come, Olivia," he said almost brusquely. "Let us return to the manor. I have much to think about."

The lines of his face were hard and tense and his stride aggressive. Liv's heart sank. She'd made a terrible mistake in confessing her love. Maybe she'd risked her life for him, but this was 1796, not 1996. As far as Gabriel was concerned, she was a servant girl. As lord of the manor, he might take her to his bed, but he would never love her. Certainly not forever. With great sadness, she followed Gabriel toward his home.

8

GABRIEL WALKED quickly down the hall to the library, and Liv followed, still unsure of his mood. When he placed the jewels on his desk, she took the opportunity to ask, "Shall I examine them more closely?"

He opened a drawer and removed a magnifying glass, which he handed to her without a word.

Trying not to be intimidated by his silence, she looked through the glass. For a moment, she forgot everything but the beauty of the stones, hardly believing their radiance.

He watched for a long time before asking, "Will you be able to restore them to their original settings?"

"They're the finest jewels I've ever seen. I'd like to reset them, but unless I have the right tools, I don't think it's possible."

"Then I must make it possible," he said quietly.

"But the tools—"

"They can be sent from London, or I will fetch them myself if necessary. I will not rest comfortably until the Stratton jewels are back in their proper settings."

"I'll do what I can, but do you think Caroline will care how they're set? If she knew the whole story..." Liv looked up at him. "I think you should tell her, Gabriel—"

She bit back the words. It wasn't her place to give advice, or even make suggestions, and she'd said too much already. The tension between them was almost palpable as he stared down with hard dark eyes that seemed to see right through her. His face wore a strained look; the same frown she'd noticed earlier creased his forward.

She stood up quickly, nervously. "I'm sorry I can't be more help with the jewels. Maybe when we get the tools . . ."

He shrugged. "That is not what is important now. That can wait while we talk about other matters which must be addressed."

Her heart caught in her throat. What was he going to tell her? She thought she knew. That what had happened between them was over. And when the jewels were set, he would ask her to leave.

No! She refused to believe her own suspicions. Their attraction was too great, their feelings too strong to be so easily dismissed.

"I have made a decision, Olivia."

She looked at him and caught her breath.

"I am going to put an end to this," he said.

Her world collapsed. For an instant, she stood motionless and then moved away from him, slowly at first and then faster, crossing the room, through the door and into the hall.

"Where are you going?" he called after her.

She didn't answer as she continued to walk away, down the hall, past the gallery of family portraits—past *his* portrait—to the vast marble foyer. She wouldn't listen to what he was telling her. She didn't want him to turn her away. This was her fantasy, and she wasn't ready to let it go.

"Olivia!" He ran after her, catching up as she reached the huge front door and grabbing her by the arm.

"If you do not stop this nonsensical behavior, I will put you over my knee and give you a good spanking."

She turned toward him, more hurt than angry. "I can't think why you're making a joke of all this."

"I am not making a joke, Olivia."

"Then if you're serious, you must realize the lord of the manor can't be seen chasing after a servant."

"I have told you, Olivia, I make the rules here. At Northcliffe Manor, 'Nice customs do curtsy to great barons—or kings,' as the Bard said."

"This isn't the time for Shakespeare."

He took her arm again and pulled her after him, down the hall. "I have no idea why you are suddenly behaving like this, but I will not have it."

"It's not your choice, I'm afraid. I come from a time where men don't make all the rules." She tried to get away from him, but he held fast, pulling her along until they reached the library.

"Sit down," he commanded, leading her to the desk chair.

Giving him a dirty look, she sat.

He pulled up another chair next to her. "I have no idea what is the matter with you, Olivia. Nor why we are arguing. I have something I want to tell you and—"

She put her hands over her ears. "I don't want to hear."

"I cannot imagine why not. This is what you have asked of me."

She dropped her hands. "What are you talking about?"

"You have been right about the Highwayman."

She gasped audibly. "*That's* what you wanted to tell me?"

"Yes," he said. "It is difficult for me to admit, but is it not what you have believed all along?"

"I—I thought you were going to tell me something else, something about us. That you wanted to end this—our—"

"My Olivia, what are you saying? Of course not."

"But you were so serious and distant."

"Yes, I have been troubled. About my role." He moved to the fireplace. The flames cast dancing lights and shadows across his face. For the first time, she noticed the vulnerability there. He drew in a deep breath.

"I convinced myself that my purpose was noble when I rode as the Highwayman, but I realize now that I have been reckless and foolish, possibly even wrong, to set myself up as judge of the men who cheated my father. What they did was dishonest and evil, but my father allowed it to happen. To avenge his name, I stole from them and used the money to restore my heritage."

He shook his head in frustration. "I told myself that I was seeking justice, but all I cared about was vengeance. I wanted to hurt others as they'd hurt my father, and through him, our family. I had room for nothing in my heart but hate and revenge."

"And now?" Her throat was dry, her words a whisper.

He took her hand. "Now, my sweet Olivia, I have room in my heart for no one except you."

And she had imagined he didn't want her anymore! She felt as if her own heart would burst with joy.

He leaned close and looked into her eyes. "I swear to you that I shall never ride as the Highwayman again."

"Oh, I'm so glad. And all this time, I thought—"

"Pray, go on," he urged. "You can say anything to me, Olivia." He grinned. "You usually do."

She took a deep breath. "I was afraid that we could never be together because of the differences between us. In your world, I'm only a servant in the house of a great nobleman."

He burst into laughter. "But you rarely treat me with the deference my title deserves, and God knows, you have never had the manner of a serving wench." He touched her cheek lightly. "I care nothing about your position in society. As always, I do as I wish, not as others dictate."

"But—"

He put his finger on her lips. "There is nothing more to say. We are together, and I have you to love and to care for and to worry about—"

"Say that again," she begged.

"That I worry about you?" He raised his eyebrows ingenuously.

"No, Gabriel, that you love me."

He stood up and pulled her from the chair into his arms. "Yes, I love you, Olivia." He kissed her passionately, and she wrapped her arms around his neck, pressing her body close to his. She felt his tongue on hers and lost herself in his kiss.

He loved her! "When did you know?" she whispered. "That you loved me?"

He laughed softly. "Must I name a day and hour?"

"And minute," she demanded.

He held her close. "You ask such unusual questions. I will try to answer, but I must think about this for a long time," he teased.

"No, answer quickly, without thinking about it."

"All right. Perhaps the moment when I first saw you."

"In the tavern? Never! You were much too preoccupied."

"The moment we first kissed . . ."

"I don't think so. You regarded me as a servant then."

He laughed loudly, hugging her all the while. "As usual, you ask me a question and then refute my answers. So I will tell you. Today. When I realized that you had risked your life for me and I might have lost you."

"But I thought you were angry at me."

"There was much on my mind, and I *was* angry with you—for so foolishly endangering yourself. But I was more angry at myself for thinking I could play the Highwayman forever without retribution—to myself or to those I love." He held her face in his hands. "And to be honest, I was frightened when I thought of my love for you."

"Afraid? You, the brave Baron Northcliffe?"

"I have never before loved a woman, certainly never expressed my love. There was such a tumult of emotions, such confusion." He smiled at her. "I still find my feelings difficult to express."

"You do it very well, my darling. Just three little words. 'I love you.'"

"I love you," he said slowly. "The words are not so difficult. Indeed, they are pleasing to my tongue."

"And to my ears," she said, snuggling against him with a sigh. "I'm so glad that our careers as the Highwayman...I mean the Highwayperson...are over. We have the jewels."

"Because of your actions—and your cleverness—the Highwayman shall not ride again. I vow it, Olivia. Northcliffe Manor will survive. And as we build up our stables, we will become what we once were in my grandfather's day. If I fail in one way, I will succeed in another," he vowed.

"I've never doubted your resourcefulness, my love. Just as I would never argue about your stubbornness and courage."

She'd known Gabriel for such a short time that it seemed impossible for her feelings to be so deep and strong. But they were. It was as if the two of them were bound together, not by days but by years of shared emotions. Yet she knew it could all be over in a flash. "Oh, Gabe, I can't bear the thought of losing you." She touched his face tenderly.

"You will never lose me, Olivia. Now, come, let us sit beside the fire and talk."

She took his hand and let him lead her to the divan in front of the fireplace, where they settled comfortably. "I vow to you, my Olivia," he said, putting his arm around her shoulders, "never to do anything more dangerous than having an argument with you."

"That's not what I mean, Gabe. It's not your riding as the Highwayman, although that's part of it. This is also about me. I don't know how long I can stay here. What if I'm suddenly snatched back to the future? The book may have brought me here, but some other force could take me away."

He closed his eyes, and rested his head back. "You still persist . . ."

"Yes, I persist, and the pepper spray gives credence to my story. It's a twentieth-century invention, Gabe. And what about me, the way I look and talk? The things I know about, events that haven't even happened yet? Why won't you believe me?" She sighed deeply. "Who do you think I am? Tell me, Gabe," she demanded.

He opened his eyes and met her gaze directly. "You are a brave and intelligent woman. I think that you may be from America, as you say. That would account for much in your speech and actions. And I am beginning to think that you were sent to me—by something, someone, unknown—to help me change my ways." He seemed satisfied with this deduction.

She couldn't control her frustration. "But you won't accept the fact that I'm from the future!"

He sighed. "I am not sure what to accept other than that a power greater than us both has brought us together. You insist that a horseless carriage and a magic book brought you from another time. I do not doubt your sincerity, and yet—"

"You think I'm crazy!"

"No, you are confused, just as I am."

"Of course I'm confused. Who wouldn't be after traveling through time! But I'm upset, too, that you won't believe me."

His jaw tightened. "Think for a moment of what you are asking me, Olivia, to believe in something that cannot be possible."

"It's possible now," she responded, almost irritably. Then she stopped herself. Why should he believe her? If he'd come into the twentieth century with such a story, she wouldn't have believed *him*—unless he'd been able to prove it more certainly than she'd done so far. "If you let me tell you about the future, I can convince you."

"And if you do convince me, what happens to us then, Olivia?"

"What do you mean?"

"If I believe all that you have told me about your journey from the future, must I believe the rest—that what you read in the book is true, that I will die within the year?" He smiled sadly. "This I refuse to believe. I am not going to die, not when I have just found you."

"But things are different now," she argued. "You're no longer the Highwayman. We can change history."

"No one can do that, Olivia," he said firmly. "No one."

She clutched his arms and held on tightly, looking deep into his eyes. "If we love each other enough, we can," she insisted. "That's why I'm here with you. To love you and keep you safe." She dug her fingers into his muscles. "I know how we can do that, Gabe. Once we find out who committed the murders—"

"No, you must not become involved in those terrible deeds, Olivia." His voice was low but resolute. "Leave the villain to me."

"I can't help it, Gabe. We may not have much time."

"And I refuse to spend any more of it in argument."

"But, Gabe—"

"Shh, Olivia. We will talk later about this problem. It is not for now."

"But any moment—"

"No, my will is stronger than any power to take you away. And my love is greater by far. Trust me, Olivia. I will not die, and you will not be taken from me." He kissed her softly, moving his hand down her shoulder. "I have other things on my mind for you and me."

He slipped his hand under her blouse, and she felt his warm fingers against her back. "You are about to burst out of my sister's riding habit. I see no reason for you to keep it on any longer."

He nuzzled her neck, and his breath was feathery and warm against her skin. Thoughts of the future were fast disappearing. "You're changing the subject," she said weakly.

"And you like the change."

"Yes," she said with a long sigh. She slid out of the constricting blouse and tossed it on the floor. Gabriel cupped her breasts, massaging her nipples lightly with his thumbs. She could feel her breasts swell with pleasure, her nipples tighten and grow hard.

"I see you have given up that *brazier* contraption," he said with a satisfied smile.

"Mmm, your time is my time now. I'm a woman of the eighteenth century, complete with chemise and drawstring undies."

He laughed. "Undies?"

"Drawers," she corrected herself.

"Ah, yes, and their drawstring makes seduction much easier for me." He kissed her neck and the hollow between her breasts. Through the thin fabric of her eighteenth-century chemise he suckled one and then the other taut, engorged nipple. She arched toward him, her skin hot, damp and flushed with desire.

His lips still on her breast, he pushed up her skirt and insinuated his hand beneath the cotton drawers, caressing the smoothness of her thighs until he found her secret warmth. As he stroked her, his fingers worked their magic, causing a sweet melting heat to engulf her.

Liv reacted instinctively, reaching up to find his lips and kiss him long and hard. His tongue mated with hers, thrust, withdrew, and then thrust again, possessively, purposefully.

"We'll never make it to your bed, Gabe." Her voice was shaky with desire.

"Beds are for lovers from your twentieth century. In this time, we have a warm fire and a soft Turkish rug." He lifted her in his arms and settled her in front of the fire. As promised, the rug felt soft beneath her clothes— which he removed very quickly, chuckling as he pulled the string of her drawers.

Liv leaned back on her elbows to watch Gabriel undress, all the while wondering if there was any man more perfect than her lover. He peeled off his soft white shirt to reveal broad shoulders, strong chest, flat abdomen and tapering waist. She waited, the half smile on her face barely concealing her breathlessness as he unbuttoned his breeches and pulled them down over his lean hips, hard muscular thighs and strong calves.

By the time he got the trousers off, her gaze had moved back up and settled on his erect manhood. She wasn't ashamed of looking at him or of her desire for him. Gabe was hers and she loved him. She was damn well going to look. In fact, she was going to do more than look.

She grasped his ankle. "Don't go away."

"I have no plan to go anywhere," he replied.

"I'm going to drive you wild tonight, my baron." She moved her hands up his leg.

"Can a man ask for a more passionate woman?"

Liv grinned up at him. "Sometimes women of my century are accused of being too assertive." She saw the look of puzzlement on his face. "Aggressive. Physical." She moved her hands over his knee and up his thigh.

"I am not sure I understand," he said, all innocence.

"Oh, you understand, Sir Gabe! You just want to be shown, don't you? I'm the woman to do that."

"You are doing it now, Olivia. Whatever you are doing," he adding, looking down at her from his great height.

"You mean this?" She raised herself to her knees as she moved her hands again, up his thigh, close, very close to his manhood. She waited a moment before touching him, gently but firmly. She heard his quick intake of breath and looked up at him through her thick fall of hair.

His head was tilted to one side, his eyes closed, a sensuous smile playing on his lips. "You like that, my love?" she asked.

First came a little moan and then his eyes opened. He buried his hands in her hair and tilted her head back so he could see her better. "I believe I am beginning to understand this assertiveness," he said huskily.

"Just wait," she promised as she grasped his erection more firmly, stroked, caressed, feeling him grow and swell under her touch. And then her mouth was on him, hot and slick. He thought that he would ignite into flames as her lips caused an exquisite torture, pushing him to the edge of passion.

"Enough," he cried. He sank onto his knees beside her. "Another moment, and you would have driven me over the edge, my darling Olivia. For that, I want to be inside you."

His breath came in harsh rough gasps as he closed his arms around her, almost roughly, and claimed her mouth with kisses that were urgent, demanding and greedy.

"I love you, Gabe," she murmured between kisses as they fell back together onto the rug, rolling over until he was on top of her and her legs were wrapped around his back. She dug her fingers into the straining muscles of his shoulders and lifted herself toward him, eager, ready.

He slipped inside her, savoring her sweet honeyed warmth. All he could think of was loving her and giving her pleasure. He wanted to possess her, not only in body, but heart and soul.

Her eyes met his. They were bluer than a summer sky, filled with love and hope, and his heart lurched madly in his chest. He wanted to show her with his body that he loved her as he had loved no other.

Olivia. He had been waiting all his life for her, and now she was his.

THE REMAINS of a late-night supper were carelessly piled on a table in Gabriel's bedroom. He had ordered the meal and then asked his valet to have the servants prepare a bath. The copper tub was by the fire, filled with steaming water, which had been carried up bucket by bucket from the kitchen.

Wrapped in one of his silk robes, her hair piled on her head, Liv tested the water temperature. "Just right," she judged, looking at him with an impish grin. "And for once, I'm not going to talk about my century and hot and cold running water—"

"We have that in England, too," Gabe announced. "And one day I will take you with me to Bath where we will take the warm mineral waters." He untied the sash of her robe. "It is healthful but not romantic," he added, pulling off the robe and tossing it across a chair.

Liv had lost all sense of modesty. She and Gabe had explored each other's bodies so completely that there was no embarrassment in being naked before him. In fact, from the beginning there never had been. "Are you going to bathe me?" she asked.

"From head to toe." He perused her slowly for a long moment, letting his eyes dwell on her breasts.

"That sounds positively sinful." She felt a warm tingle of desire blossom inside and wondered how it was possible to want him again so soon.

She took his hand, and he helped her into the oval-shaped tub. The steam curled around her as she sank back in the deliciously warm water. It covered her legs and hips and lapped at her breasts. Closing her eyes, Liv relaxed totally.

After a few minutes luxuriating, she said dreamily, "I have an idea, Gabe."

"For some reason, that alarms me," he teased.

"This is a sensible one. Why don't we leave the Highwayman and the murders behind and emigrate to America? We could start a new life there." She didn't say what she was thinking: *If only whatever power brought her back in time would allow her to stay.* But even if she couldn't stay with him in the America of the eighteenth century, even if she were propelled back to the future, he'd be safe there, away from his enemies.

"I cannot leave here and go to America, Olivia. I must stay here and return Northcliffe Manor to its former greatness, not only for my children but for all the generations to follow."

"If you're hanged for highway robbery—or murder—nothing will follow at all."

He pulled a stool up beside the tub. "I will not be hanged, Olivia. Now give me the sponge and lean forward. You are much too slow in the bath."

That was called denial, Liv thought as he washed her back with slow even strokes. A shrink would have a field day with Gabe's defensiveness, but of course, psychiatry hadn't been invented yet, and it would be foolish for someone who'd traveled back in time to start analyzing the person who didn't believe it could happen. If anyone looked crazy here, she was the one.

"I don't want to go back to the twentieth century without you," she whispered.

"Then forget the future, Olivia. Wipe your mind clear of it."

"I can't, because it's true! And real." She knew he didn't believe her, but she couldn't let the subject drop. "It's my world—or at least it was."

"Would I be happy in your world?" Why not humor her, he mused, when she seemed so determined to talk about this place in the future and seemed convinced that it existed. He rolled up the sleeve of his robe and slipped a hand under the water. Slowly, he stroked the sponge along her legs. He'd never known a woman with legs so long or slender. He smiled to himself. Her limbs weren't all that was wonderfully different about Olivia. From head to toe, inside and out, she was unlike any woman in the world, he thought as he tried to concentrate on her answer.

"You'd fit into any world," she said staunchly. "I've known that from the first. I'd love to show you New York City—"

"Is it like London?"

"Well, I'm not sure what New York was like in 1796, but two hundred years later, it's filled with skyscrapers."

"Sky-scrapers?" he asked haltingly as he continued to move the sponge along her smooth body.

"Just like it sounds—buildings that reach the sky, forty, fifty, sixty stories high and more. A couple of them are over a hundred stories high. Streets filled with those automobiles I told you about."

"Oh, yes, your horseless carriages."

"Here are some other things you've never heard of—neon signs, electric stoplights, jackhammers—lots of those in New York City because they're always tearing down buildings and putting them back up—earth movers, even moving stairs that are called escalators, elevators, washing machines, dishwashers." She stopped and took a breath. "I could go on forever naming things—"

"With words that make no sense to me," he interrupted.

"I know. It's hard to explain." Especially, she thought, with his hand on her leg, provocative and tantalizing, sliding from ankle to knee, up and down.

"Is life better there?"

She paused before answering. "Better and worse. It can be very stressful because of the fast pace, but overall it's easier with machines doing all the work for us—" She broke off her sentence again. He'd moved the sponge to the tender flesh of her inner thigh and all she could think about was his touch.

"It sounds interesting, having a machine do your work." Gabe resoaped the sponge and moved it over her upper body. "It also sounds ridiculous." He wasn't interested in the future. Right now, he was preoccupied thinking about her body beneath the shimmering water, and his desire for it. He could feel his muscles tense with expectation.

"Sometimes it *is* ridiculous," she answered. "And sometimes it's even dangerous. But mostly life is still the same. Men and women meet and fall in love no matter what year it is. Love is as important in my time as it is in yours."

He felt that love deep inside as he touched her, and it seemed like a miracle. "You could be happy with me, Olivia. Here in my time." Gabriel's voice was low and coaxing. He began soaping her breasts, watching the expression on her face. Her eyes closed and she tilted back her head, exposing her nipples at the water line. He couldn't resist cupping her breasts in his hands.

"I could be happy with you anytime, darling Gabe." Her voice was slow and slightly slurred with pleasure.

He stood up suddenly, kicking the stool aside. The desire building inside him could no longer be controlled.

She opened her eyes. "What are you doing?"

Gabe flung his robe to the floor. "I thought I would take a bath." He stepped into the tub.

"Gabe! It's overflowing . . . Water is sloshing—"

He knelt across her hips and put his arms around her shoulders. His lips were an inch from hers. "Before we finish, sweet Olivia, there is going to be a tidal wave of mammoth proportions in this bedroom."

She leaned forward and touched his lips with hers. "Whatever you say, milord."

OLIVIA AWOKE the next morning in a tangle of bed-clothes. Gabriel lay next to her, his large body sprawled possessively over most of the bed. He was still asleep but something had wakened her. The clamor of horses? The sound of voices?

She slipped from bed and found a robe. There was more noise now, men talking, heavy footsteps coming along the hallway. Something was wrong.

She shook Gabriel's shoulder. "Wake up, Gabe! Someone is in the house."

He was instantly alert, swinging his feet to the floor. He pushed back his tangled hair and reached for a pair of breeches. Just as he buttoned them, someone pounded on the bedroom door. Then a voice boomed out.

"Gabriel Stratton, Twelfth Baron Northcliffe, in the name of His Majesty King George the Third and the Sheriff of Haroldsgate, I demand entrance."

Liv's eyes met Gabriel's and cold fear clutched her heart. The future was upon them.

The door was flung open and four men burst into the room. Gabriel continued to button his shirt and pull on his boots. His face wore a look of absolute contempt for the interlopers—and not a modicum of fear.

A short, slender and elegantly clad man stepped forward. "You are to come with me, Northcliffe," he pronounced grandly in a high nasal voice.

"I hardly think so, Fremont."

The little man's smile was triumphantly snide. "I believe you will. I have a warrant for your arrest, signed by the chief magistrate himself."

Liv clutched Gabe's robe tightly around her neck. Her nightmare was coming true.

Gabe remained cool and unshaken. "Arrest? May I ask why?"

The sheriff withdrew a folded paper from his waistcoat pocket. "For the murder of a woman named Ginny Collins."

Liv gasped and clapped her hand across her mouth. For murder!

"I know no one of that name," Gabriel said firmly.

"Perhaps not, but you murdered her. A silk handkerchief bearing your initial was found beneath the body." Fremont's voice was oily smooth.

"That is not possible," Gabriel replied.

Liv remembered her first day at Northcliffe; Gabe had offered her one of his silk handkerchiefs. The monogram was unmistakable. But how had it gotten to the murder scene?

"She was murdered last night, strangled, just as the others before her," Fremont said.

Liv let out a big audible sigh. All eyes focused on her. "Last night he was with me! All night. In that bed." She pointed dramatically. "I can give him an alibi. Someone planted the handkerchief."

"Olivia, stay out of this," Gabe warned in a low voice.

He was overridden by Fremont, who looked her coolly up and down. His tone was derisive. "And who are you? His mistress, some wench he has taken to his bed? We have no reason to believe a personage such as yourself."

Gabriel made his move then, surging forward and grabbing the sheriff by the satin lapels of his coat. "You slimy bastard, you vile piece of excrement. You are not fit to be in the same room with her—"

"Arrest him!" the sheriff screamed. "Arrest this man. He is as mad as his father before him!"

Two of the men grabbed Gabriel's arms and pulled him away from the very ruffled Fremont. But the baron was still fighting, twisting and turning violently, and a third officer joined in to help subdue him.

"Let him go," Liv screamed, lunging forward and swinging at the men. "You can't do this! He was with me. He's innocent!"

The sheriff snatched her by the hair and gave a mighty pull. Olivia shrieked and fell back on the floor, the breath knocked from her body. "Take him away," Fremont ordered. "He will be judged by his peers."

As the guards dragged Gabe out of the room and down the hall, Olivia struggled to her feet and staggered after them.

Gabe continued to fight like a wild man, pulling and thrashing. He kicked out and connected with one of his guards, his foot crunching into the man's groin, causing him to double over with a painful cry.

"Control the wild animal!" the sheriff cried, but Gabe fought even harder, almost breaking loose at the top of the stairs.

The sheriff acted quickly. He grabbed a musket from one of the men and brought the butt down savagely on the side of Gabe's head.

Liv saw the blood spurt from the jagged wound. "No! Gabe, oh, Gabe," she cried, staggering toward them, while from behind partially closed doors, the servants cowered, powerless and afraid to intervene.

She reached the stairs as the men struggled down them with Gabe's inert body. The sheriff looked back at her with a sneer on his face as she leaned over the stairwell, shaking her fist.

"You'll never be able to hold Gabriel Stratton in your jail," she screamed. "He'll outsmart you all. Just wait, you'll see!" Her voice echoed hollowly in the huge dome of the entrance hall.

She sank onto the floor, watching through the stair rails, sobbing. As the door slammed behind the four men and her lover, Liv made a promise to herself. "I'll help you, Gabe. Somehow, you'll be freed. Somehow..."

9

GABRIEL'S CELL was barely six by eight feet, a small dark chamber with a floor covered by dirty straw. There was no window. The only light came from a smoking torch in the dank hall outside the cell. The stench of rot was pervasive. Insects crawled the walls and rodents nestled in corners.

All of that he sensed during the first hour while he lay on the floor, half-conscious, trying to gain enough strength to get up. Finally, he struggled to a sitting position and leaned back against the wall. The pain in his head was agonizing, but he was no longer bleeding from the wound inflicted by Fremont. He forced himself to concentrate on his situation, not daring to close his eyes for fear he would lose consciousness again.

Some time later, he heard a rumbling noise outside. It sounded as if a crowd had gathered near the building. Men were yelling and pounding on the jailhouse door. As he tried to clear his head, the noise grew louder, the banging more violent. He stood up and went to the gate but could see nothing. The faintly lit hall led to the guardroom, which was blocked from his view by a heavy door.

Then he heard Fremont's voice above the noise of the crowd, and after a short while, silence.

There was no way to judge the passing of time, but most of the day must have gone by because a guard had come to the cell door twice with what passed for his meals—first, a portion of meat not fit for a dog, and moldy bread; later, watery tea and some kind of gruel. He refused the first meal, but by the time the sickening gruel arrived, he did more than decline—he threw it back at the guard. It splattered over the other man's face, causing violent curses and threats of a beating. Gabriel faced the tall, scrawny man through the bars, daring him to open the door.

If only he could have gotten the guard inside his cell, even in his weakened condition, Gabriel would have been able to subdue him. That had been his hope, but he never got an opportunity to carry out his plan. The man backed away with no more than a snarl. He wore no sidearms, but Gabriel knew there were muskets nearby, primed and ready, in the guardroom. And next time, if the guard decided to open the cell door, the man would be armed.

The next morning, Gabriel had the sickening feeling that he'd missed his only chance. The cell door was the only way out of this small, windowless room that was his prison. And the guards, at least, weren't going to open it unarmed. As that thought swam in his head, he heard the sound of the door to the guardroom opening, followed by footsteps. And then he saw her.

"Olivia!" Her name was a blessing on his lips.

She was dressed neatly in her brown maid's uniform and crisp white apron, her glorious hair bound carefully into a chignon. She looked pale and anxious. He put his hand over his wound to hide it from her, but she'd already seen it and let out a gasp.

"I've brought clothing," she said, and Gabriel noted the bundle she clutched. Turning to the guard, she said, "You promised to leave us alone when I gave you the money. Please, keep your word. I'll only be a few minutes, and you can watch from the door."

Gabriel was careful not to look in the man's direction, fearful that his glare would ignite anger. Finally, the guard moved away to the end of the hall.

Liv grasped Gabe's hand through the bars and held it to her cheek. "Thank God, you're alive. I was afraid they'd killed you. But your head—"

"It is all right. Do not worry." He could think of nothing but her touch, which sent a rush of joy through him. He ran his fingers along her cheek and across her lips. Seeing her, touching her was like water to a man dying of thirst. Her skin was silky soft, and the sweet scent of her filled his nostrils.

"I can't believe they've beaten you and locked you in this terrible place, Gabe. You're a nobleman. They can't keep you here."

His jaw tightened. "I once believed that myself, but it seems we have both been misinformed. They are proving without a doubt that they *can* keep me here. Bribery can only achieve so much, and I see you have used that ploy."

She nodded. "It took all the money Caroline had for me to get in here with your clothes." She thrust them through the bars.

"Can I hope there is a pistol tucked in a pocket?" he asked with attempted lightness.

"There isn't. The guard checked. But I considered the old file-in-the-cake routine."

"File in the cake?"

"I'll explain later." She held his hand tightly. "We don't have long, Gabe. The sheriff could appear at any minute. We have to make plans to get you out of here. Do you have a lawyer?"

"The family barrister is in London, but I doubt he can be reached in time."

"Of course he can. The trial won't be held immediately."

"There may not be a trial, Olivia."

"I don't understand."

"Their kind of justice may be much swifter," he said. "Yesterday, Fremont apparently dispersed a crowd outside the jail."

"What about it?"

"Just this. By now, everyone has heard that I have been arrested for killing Ginny Collins. They probably believe I murdered the other women, as well, and they have begun to band together. I imagine that John Darcy and his friends are at the Boot and Bottle planning a second siege on the jail. They are eager to see me hanged, Olivia. My handkerchief is the proof they have been waiting for."

"The handkerchief was planted, Gabe! All we have to do is find the real murderer."

"I am afraid there is not time." He saw her face grow pale, and he tightened his grip on her trembling hands. "It seems as though I was wrong about the future. Baron Northcliffe *will* be hanged as you read, in the year 1796. Unless a miracle occurs."

"Miracles happen. We're a miracle! Don't give up, my darling." Her face felt tight as she fought to hold back her tears. She couldn't let him see her cry. She had to be brave for Gabriel, but inside she felt as if her heart were breaking into a thousand pieces.

Reaching through the bars, Gabe pushed a strand of hair from her face. "Oh, my sweet Olivia," he said softly, "I must believe now that you *were* sent from another time to warn me. You told me again and again, but I refused to listen."

"It's not too late," Liv insisted. "We can still do something—"

"No, Olivia. I am willing to accept my fate, the fate you warned me of so often. What concerns me is not myself but you and Caroline. What does she know?"

"Everything," Liv answered bluntly.

Gabriel swore under his breath.

"And she understands." Caroline had cried at first when Liv told her about Gabe's deeds as the Highwayman, the jewels and his arrest. Then she'd surprised both Liv and Michael with her steeliness and resolve. Now, Liv could swear that Caroline would be willing to risk anything to free her brother. "She isn't afraid, Gabe. She's strong and brave—"

"She does not understand what is happening, Olivia, just as you did not until you came here. There will be no lawyer, no trial, nothing. *There is not time*. Caro will not be safe in Northcliffe Manor, and you must get her away from there. Do this for me, Olivia—take her to my aunt in Bath."

Liv shook her head. "Caroline has plans of her own. She and Michael—"

"Michael?"

"Have you been blind or just in denial? Well, it doesn't matter," she said dismissively. "He's in love with her and she's in love with him, and—"

Gabe started to speak, but Liv put her fingers over his lips. "Stop and think, Gabe. Look at us, a nobleman and a serving wench. You say that doesn't matter. Then why should Michael and Caroline be different?"

"She is my little sister—"

"He loves her, Gabe. And more importantly, he'll protect her. She'll be safer with Michael than with anyone's aunt."

Gabe sighed. "Then I must be thankful for that."

"Soon, we'll have much more to be thankful for, when all this is over and we're together."

Gabe couldn't conceal his frustration. "Olivia, I am in jail. I may be hanged by an angry mob within the day unless I can come up with a miracle."

"As I've said before, miracles are possible. They just need a little nudge occasionally."

"What does that mean?" You are not thinking up another harebrained scheme . . ."

She decided it was best to remain silent.

"Olivia, I will not have it!"

"What?" she asked innocently. "We've done nothing."

"We? Do not tell me you and Caroline are involved in something foolish."

"Shh, the guard will hear you."

"Olivia, I will not stand for this. The women I love most in the world must be kept safe."

"We'll be safe, but we won't see you hanged," she whispered.

"You cannot change history," he said wearily. "My being in jail proves that. And I would rather die than have anything happen to you."

"To hell with history! There's no power in the past or future that can keep us apart. I will not let you die." She felt the hot sting of tears on her lids and pressed her face against the bars, trying to touch his lips with hers. "I love you, Gabe, and I'll never let you go."

"And I love you, Olivia, with all my heart. That is why I want you to protect yourself. See that my sister is safe with Michael and then try to return to your twentieth century."

"Even if I knew for certain how to do that, I wouldn't. Not now." She heard the guard returning and lowered her voice, speaking quickly. "You're going to be free, Gabriel. I swear it."

"Leave that to me," he begged helplessly, knowing he would never get out on his own but determined that she and Caroline not put their lives at risk. "Promise me, Olivia."

"Wench, ye best be leavin'," the guard called out. "'Tis time for the new shift, and I can't be responsible."

"Promise, Olivia," Gabe insisted, holding her hand so tightly she thought he might crush her bones.

"I promise," she said softly.

He breathed a deep sigh. "Now kiss me farewell. Our last kiss, one that will last me to eternity."

OLIVIA KNEW that Gabe was right. She was putting herself, Caroline and even Michael in jeopardy. But she had to do it. They'd all talked it over and realized there was no other choice. The plan had been put together quickly but carefully. And the time was now.

She felt a drop of perspiration roll down her face and wished she had a free hand to wipe it away. She tried to focus on what Caroline was saying to the guard.

"Of course I have permission from Sheriff Fremont to visit my brother. To bring him a decent meal." She indicated the cooking pot that Liv held. "And to allow him time to talk with his clergyman."

The shift had changed and there was a new guard, burly with a potbelly. He scratched his scraggly beard. "The sheriff didn't say naught to me—"

"I am sure he did not," Caroline replied imperiously. "But he did write a letter of permission." She pulled the paper out of her sleeve. "See, here it is. Signed by the high sheriff." She waved the letter under his eyes.

Liv held her breath and prayed. She'd labored for an hour over the fake letter, but Caroline had declared that the contents really didn't matter because the guards probably couldn't read. Liv hoped she was right.

The guard seemed to waver. He was paying more attention to the words of the elegantly gowned lady before him than to the letter. A good sign, Liv thought.

"More importantly," Caroline went on, "a man of the cloth is waiting outside. I cannot believe you will not allow my brother a chance to cleanse his soul."

A second guard appeared in the door, a somewhat older man with a dirt-streaked face and watery eyes. Liv recognized him at once as Clovis, the man who'd harassed her in the tavern. She ducked her head.

"What's all the noise, Jack?" he asked.

The guard named Jack seemed relieved to share the problem. "'Er ladyship 'as a letter from the sheriff to visit the baron. And she says there's a clergyman waiting outside. Hit's all writ out in a letter," he added.

"Hmm." Clovis took the letter and studied it, whether intelligently or not, Liv couldn't be sure. But he was obviously indecisive. If the letter wasn't genuine and he let them in, he would be in trouble. On the other hand, if it was real and he ignored the high sheriff's order...

"Two women and a rector," he mused aloud. "I don't reckon they'll cause any problems."

"Thank you," Caroline said, nodding graciously. "I will fetch the Reverend Mr. Brighton."

Liv kept her head low, watching out of the corner of her eye as Caroline stepped outside and Clovis moved closer.

"Don't I know ye, wench?"

"Me? I don't think so—"

"'Deed I do. Ye're the one from the tavern, the serving wench. Got yerself a fine job, eh?"

"Not so fine. Just a day's honest work."

"Well, ye'll be out o' work agin 'cause the baron will be hangin' in the gallows soon enow. As God made green apples, the baron is a murderer."

Liv bit back a retort about "being innocent until proven guilty." "It means naught to me," she lied, relieved that Caroline had reentered the jail, followed by the reverend, bent over, shuffling, dressed in a rusty black suit.

Suspicion flickered in Clovis's piglike eyes. "He ain't the rector from the village church."

"Certainly not," Caroline answered spiritedly. "He is an old friend of our family who has traveled a great distance to be with the baron." She took the elderly man's arm. "And now, if you will let us pass. Olivia, follow me and be careful with that stew."

Olivia was amazed to see both Clovis and Jack step out of the way as Caroline and the old man swept into the cell area. Quickly, she darted behind them with the pot of stew.

Gabriel's mouth fell open at the parade that greeted him. "Caro, my God! What are you doing here?"

"I've come to visit you and to bring Mr. Brighton, the beloved clergyman of your childhood. Remember?"

Olivia saw the puzzlement in Gabriel's eyes as he scoped out the old man shuffling toward his cell. The clergyman's suit was loose and baggy, and strands of gray hair straggled from under his hat.

"Is it not lovely to see the rector again?" Caroline chattered brightly on while Clovis and Jack hovered nearby. "Olivia has brought some of Cook's wonderful rabbit stew."

Olivia set the pot down near the cell and quickly slipped one hand into her pocket. There it was. Her trusty pepper spray, ready for the right moment. She tensed, poised on the balls of her feet, ready to spring into action. It was almost time.

Caroline raised her innocent eyes to Jack. "Could you unlock my brother's cell so that the reverend and I can speak privately with him?"

Suddenly, the reverend began to speak, mouthing the lines of a poem.

"Oh, open the door, some pity to show,
Oh, open the door to me, oh!"

The obese guard started visibly at that strange outburst, but not as visibly as Gabe.

"No, your ladyship," Clovis said, stepping forward
authoritatively. "We 'ave our orders never to unlock
this cell."

"Then we will have to do something about that,
won't we?" Caroline asked in her sweet lilting voice.
"Rector?"

With that, the elderly "Mr. Brighton" straightened
to his full height and pulled a pistol from his waistband. "Hand over the key or you'll have a bullet in your
head."

"Michael," Gabe breathed.

"Olivia, strike now!" Michael called.

Liv whirled toward Jack, the pepper spray in her
hand. "Sorry, pal, but I have to do this." She pressed
the trigger. Nothing happened. She pressed again,
harder. The spray was jammed!

For a moment, he stood looking at her in amazement. Then he roared, "Out of my way, wench."

Knowing Michael had to get the keys and pass them
to Caroline as planned, Liv stood her ground, shook the
spray and tried again. Nothing!

Jack came raging forward, and Liv had no choice left.
She flung herself at him.

It was like hitting the side of a mountain. With one
huge paw, he pushed her aside, but she wasn't daunted.
She jumped on his back, holding on by grabbing his

ears. As he bucked and slapped at her, she stayed astride him and even managed to get the fingers of one hand in his eye, scratching with all her might.

With a loud cry, he backed toward the wall, and Liv knew he meant to crush her against it. She looked toward the cell. Caroline had the key!

Liv let go just before they hit the wall, and dropped to the ground.

For Gabriel, it was as if a nightmare was unfolding before his eyes, a hideous debacle in which all he loved could perish. Liv, after fighting a man three times her size, had held on like a terrier but was now on the ground, vulnerable to the brute of a guard.

Caroline put the key in the lock, pushed and pulled frantically, and then cried out, "I cannot turn it."

Michael, distracted by the panicked tone of her voice, shifted his eyes toward her and away from the other guard. In that fraction of a second, Clovis slammed him to the floor and struggled for the pistol. Michael held on to it, but Gabriel knew it wouldn't be for long.

He kept his voice as calm as possible. "Push the key all the way in, Caro. Harder. That's it. Turn to the right, now!"

As soon as he heard the click, he pulled the cell door open and bolted forward, heading for Olivia and hoping Michael could hold out a little longer. But he hadn't counted on the quick action of his sister.

As Gabe rushed forward, she picked up the pot of stew and crashed it down on Clovis's head. The guard collapsed on Michael, who managed to get out from under him and struggle to his feet.

Gabriel hurled himself on Jack, forcing him away from Olivia.

"Get out of here," he shouted. "All of you!"

Michael and Caroline flew by, but Olivia remained, glued to the spot.

Gabriel summoned all the strength he possessed and hit the huge guard again and again, amazed at the man's ability to stay on his feet. Finally, he drew back his fist, took aim and crushed it against Jack's jaw. The guard fell at last, like a mighty oak.

Gabe grabbed Olivia's arm and dragged her toward the door. "I asked for a miracle, and I got one!" he exclaimed as they ran through the guardroom and out into the night.

Caroline was in the carriage, holding the door open. As soon as Gabe pushed Olivia inside, Michael, in the driver's seat, snapped his whip. As the horses raced away, the Scotsman called out lines from another Robert Burns poem.

"A fig for those by law protected!
Liberty's a glorious treat!"

Inside the carriage, they heard his cries and laughed with relief.

"We did it," Liv said. "Oh, my God, we did it!" She covered Gabe's face with kisses. "I told you we'd never be apart."

He held her close. "You are my miracle, Olivia. But this is not over yet. The guards will raise the alarm and the whole town will be after us."

"Then come to Scotland with Michael and me," Caroline pleaded. "We will be safe there in his village. The Scots care little for English law and will protect us."

"Take Olivia with you," Gabe ordered. "I have a score to settle here."

"No way," Liv cried. "I'm not leaving you."

"Olivia, I do not want to argue—"

"Neither do I. I'm not—"

"Enough!" Caroline ordered. "You two cannot be separated any more than can Michael and I. It is senseless to argue with fate." She reached into a pouch sewn in the lining of her jacket and pulled out a glittering treasure. "The Stratton jewels. They belong to us all now. Take what you need."

"Never," Gabe said. "Those are your dowry..."

"Michael and I want to share them with you."

"No, Caro—"

"Please, I beg you. At least take the earrings," Caroline insisted, putting them in Liv's hands. "There are two rubies and two sapphires in each. They could buy your freedom, Gabriel...or passage to America."

Liv closed her fingers around the jewels. "You're sweet and generous, Caroline." She looked at Gabe. "These may save our lives."

He nodded. "Thank you, my dear sister."

Caro fought back tears. "And I thank you, Gabriel, for understanding the love Michael and I share." She still held Olivia's hand. "I believe you are responsible for that acceptance, dear Olivia." Caroline kissed her cheek softly.

"There are horses hidden in a copse of trees by the road," Caroline told her brother.

"You have thought of everything."

"Except when I will see you again." Her tears began to flow.

Gabriel took her in his arms. "You will always be in my heart, Caro, and when this is settled, we will all see each other again."

Liv spoke quietly to them. "Michael's poet, Robert Burns, has the perfect words.

'And I will come again, my love
Though it were ten thousand miles.'"

They both hugged her close. "Until then," Gabe said, "be safe, dear sister." He kissed her forehead, and Caroline clung to him.

Liv felt tears run down her cheeks. Caroline and Michael *would* be safe. And she and Gabriel would be together—at least for a while. During that time, the danger would be greater than ever.

The night was not half-over. When dawn came, would her love for Gabriel have changed history?

10

LIV FELT as if her life was coming full circle. Here she was, clinging once more to Gabriel's waist as he urged Eclipse on, faster and faster through the night. Michael had brought a horse for her, but after the experience with Gracie, she felt safer riding double behind Gabe.

She easily adapted to the rhythm and speed of the great horse and to the muscular breadth of Gabe's back. But as she pressed her body against him, she had to fight the feeling of foreboding that rose inside her.

Gabriel had only hinted at his mission, and she'd asked no questions. She was determined to go wherever it led them. Deep down she knew. It would lead to the murderer; that was the score he had to settle.

They crested a hill and he reined in the horse. Below them loomed a huge manor with gothic towers and menacing battlements. It lay like an eerie fortress in the moonlight.

"Where are we?" she asked.

He turned in the saddle to face her. "It's called Barton Keep."

"It looks deserted."

"Except for one servant, too old to be roused, the manor house has been empty for the past fortnight."

"How do you know that unless—" She paused for a moment. "This is where you come when you go charging off on Eclipse! But who are you looking for?"

Gabe swung out of the saddle and dropped to the ground. "My cousin, Viscount Tancred. This is his home."

"Jeremy Barton," she murmured, remembering her one unpleasant encounter with the man. A shiver traveled down her spine. "Gabe, do you believe he's the man who killed those poor women?"

Gabe helped Liv down and kept one arm around her. "I never trusted him, never liked him, but he was my kinsman, Olivia."

"I understand that," she said.

"I could not believe him to be a murderer, but with each terrible crime, I became more and more suspicious. Many clues pointed toward him. Perhaps he felt that I was getting too close to proving him the murderer, and that is why he has hidden from me."

"Jeremy had access to Northcliffe Manor. He stole your handkerchief and left it beside the last girl who was found dead!"

"To lead the sheriff away from him—toward me. But I have no proof."

Liv felt her pulse pound with excitement. For the first time in twenty-four hours, she was optimistic. "If we can get him to confess, your name will be cleared. You can stay at Northcliffe Manor. Caroline and Michael can return—"

Gabe quelled her excitement. "Jeremy is not going to confess to anything."

"Then we'll look for evidence in the house. Serial killers often collect trophies from the people they kill," Liv whispered, holding tightly to Gabe, grateful for his warmth in the chill of the night.

"I do not know what you mean by 'serial killers,' Olivia, but I do know that Jeremy is a murderer. Whether this can be proven or not, he must be stopped. No matter what happens to me, one way or another, Jeremy will not kill again."

Now the chill was inside Olivia, turning her skin clammy and cold. "What are you going to do?"

"I am going into the house and wait for him to return. I have been unsuccessful in confronting him thus far, but I found a way inside through an unlocked door. He will come home this time. Tonight will be different."

"How different, Gabe?"

"He will have heard of my escape and will be looking for me just as I am looking for him. When he does not find me at Northcliffe Manor, it follows that he will come here. It is between the two of us, and here I will face him. My distant cousin has much to answer for," he said grimly. "I am going in now. I want you to remain hidden away in the trees—"

"No way, Gabe! I'm not staying here alone in the dark with a serial killer at large."

"Olivia—"

"No, Gabe. I've already had one run-in with Tancred, and I won't risk another. I'm coming with you."

Gabriel sighed heavily. "Perhaps you will be safer with me. But you must promise to be careful and not take any unnecessary chances."

"I promise. Now come on," she said with mock bravery. "Let's get this show on the road."

THEY ENTERED through an unlocked door that was almost hidden on the side of the great house. After making their way in total darkness to the front chamber, Gabriel lit the tapers in a candelabra. The candlelight darted eerily around the great hall, creating looming shadows on the walls.

"What next?" she whispered, drawing closer to Gabe.

"The tower room."

The tower!" She was reminded of beheaded English royals and murdered little princes. "Gruesome."

"Perhaps," he answered as he led her quickly down a narrower hall. "But I have no weapons."

"Michael left the guard's pistol on the jailhouse floor," she remembered in dismay.

"Yes. There is a collection of armor and weapons in the tower room."

"You won't kill him, Gabe?"

"Olivia—"

"You'll just use the weapon to threaten him, get a confession so we can turn him over to the sheriff . . ."

Gabe didn't answer as they reached the tower stairs and began the upward climb with Olivia clinging to him, trying not to think of what was coming.

They entered the door on the first landing into what looked like a museum, its stone walls glistening damply in the evening chill. "It really is spooky in here, Gabe." She held on to him, trying to gain strength from his arms, but her eyes roamed the crowded walls, and what she saw was discouraging at best, a collection of rusty, unwieldy weapons.

"They look hopeless," she cried.

"Unfortunately, they are all that is available." He reached for one of a pair of dueling swords. "More than a few years old, I'll warrant, but still—"

A noise from above interrupted his words.

"Gabe! Did you hear that?" she asked in a whisper.

"I heard," he answered grimly.

"What's up there?"

"Other rooms, more dismal than this."

"Could he be hiding there, waiting for you?"

"I do not know but I am going to find out." He removed the other sword and handed it to her.

She took it gingerly. The sword was heavier than she expected.

"Do not worry. It is just for assurance while I investigate the noise."

"No, Gabe—" She heard the noise again and clung to him. "I want to go with you."

"This time you must listen to me, Olivia. If Tancred is there, he may be armed, and I will have to worry about him—not about you. Bolt the door after me, and you will be safe here." He opened the heavy door carefully, took the candelabra, kissed her quickly and was gone.

Liv watched him disappear up the stairs before closing the heavy door. She tried to slip the bolt, but it didn't move. It was rusted in place. After trying several more times, she finally gave up. Surely she'd be safe enough with Gabe between her and Tancred.

She glanced at the narrow tower-room windows. Fifteen feet above the ground. No one could get in that way. All she had to do was watch the door, sword in hand. If Tancred came through, she'd be ready for him, Liv tried to convince herself as she cut the air with the saber a couple of times. She felt confident, maybe even enough to go to Gabe's aid if he needed help.

She held her breath and waited. Was Tancred upstairs, or was it just a rat she'd heard? "Same thing," she muttered.

Gabe had left a candle behind, but it lit only a corner of the moldy room. She stayed at the door, out of the light, just in case.

There was only silence. Then suddenly, she heard a sharp noise, not from above, but from behind her. Liv's heart caught in her throat as she turned to see a figure appear from nowhere, moving slowly through the light of her candle.

"Tancred! How did you—"

He approached her, a wolfish grin on his face. "A secret panel behind the bookcase inside the walls. It opens from the floor above."

"That was the noise—"

"Of course. I know my impetuous cousin only too well. He would most certainly rush to investigate."

"He'll be back," Liv said, her voice a croak, her heart pounding a hundred miles an hour.

"Oh, yes, he will return. Just in time to find your lifeless body." He stepped closer and spoke in a hoarse whisper. "Strangling you will give me special pleasure, for I remember that day at Northcliffe Manor when you rejected me so proudly. Yes, wench, I remember," he repeated.

Liv could hardly stop her body from shaking, but she couldn't let her nerve fail her now. She had to get control of herself. Tancred hadn't seen the sword! She held it by her side, hidden in the folds of her long skirt. Her fingers were damp and sweaty on the hilt of the weapon. She prayed for courage.

"My poor foolish cousin, the brazen Northcliffe," he went on contemptuously, "making himself so vulnerable. First the rumors that he was the Highwayman, and then my own clever insinuations in the right ears that he was also a murderer. No one will mourn his death—neither nobles nor peasants—and the Northcliffe title shall fall into my heroic hands. But first—"

He took another step toward her, and she charged at him, flashing the sword. Driven by fear and desperation, she caught a stunned Tancred off guard. His hand reached for the pistol tucked into his waistband just as she stabbed out with the sword.

It caught him on the arm. "Bitch!" he cried as the pistol sailed out of his hand across the room. He started to move toward it, and she swung again. A thin line of blood appeared from his ear down his neck.

More quickly than she could believe, before she had a chance to attack with the sword again, he grabbed her, twisting her arm. The sword fell to the floor, and his hands were on her neck.

"A brave gesture, my dear. Unfortunately, only a gesture." The blood dripped from his face onto her blouse. "But one that angers me greatly."

She struggled, trying to pull away his hands, but he only held her more tightly, digging his fingers into her neck.

"You are going to die this night, my fancy wench," he threatened. "The sheriff will find your body beside that of your lover."

Liv fought harder, slapped at him, tried to kick him in the groin, but he twisted to one side, his hands still like iron around her neck.

Her air supply was almost gone. She couldn't speak or even breathe. Blackness swam in front of her eyes. She could feel his breath on her cheek.

"I shall tell the sheriff how I had to kill Northcliffe to protect myself after he strangled you. Think of history, wench! You two die—and I become a hero."

In spite of the blood roaring in her ears, she heard those terrible words and attempted one last struggle. It was hopeless. She felt the life draining from her body. She was going to die!

From far away, she heard a deep voice, the wonderful voice of her Gabriel.

"Unhand her, Tancred!"

Her assailant dropped her like a sack of flour, and she hit the floor with a jolt. Rolling over, she saw Gabe's shadowy form in the doorway.

"Say your prayers, Tancred. This is the night you meet your maker."

The viscount picked up Liv's sword. "Defend yourself, Northcliffe."

Liv pulled herself into a sitting position against the wall, her hand on her neck. Her throat was swollen and closed, and she struggled for breath as she watched the scene unfold in front of her.

Tancred's movements were swift and strong, but Gabe countered quickly as he advanced across the tower room wielding his sword with impassioned vengeance. The viscount parried each thrust expertly.

Liv was mesmerized by their movement and the sounds of clanging sword on sword and harsh breathing as the men became locked in mortal combat.

Tancred feinted, and his sword nicked Gabriel's shoulder. A bright spot of red appeared, but the blood, which startled Liv, served only to infuriate Gabe. With a low growl, he advanced toward Tancred, forcing him back. Liv could tell, even in the flickering candlelight, that Tancred was tiring fast. His thrusts and parries were those of a desperate man, and Gabe didn't give an inch. He was on him in an instant, forcing him backward against the wall.

It was over, Liv thought. Gabe had won!

And then with a mighty cry, Tancred lunged forward. Gabe, caught unaware, lost his balance. With a shriek of triumph, Tancred raised his sword and charged.

Liv grasped her throat and felt her heart stop. The candle flickered, and for a moment the men were lost in shadow. She tried to scream, but no sound came.

Suddenly, she saw Gabe. He'd slipped, almost gone down and then regained his balance. He caught the light as he turned to one side and thrust out his sword. Too late to stop his forward momentum, Tancred ran full force onto the sword and the blade drove deep into his heart. He fell at Gabe's feet.

Liv struggled from the floor and rushed into Gabe's arms. They stood over Tancred. "He's dead, isn't he?" she asked in a wavering voice.

"Yes, and not soon enough," was the bitter response.

"All the blood—"

"Do not look, Olivia."

She hid her face against his chest. "He was going to kill us both. First me, and then you."

He touched her neck, tenderly stroking the bruises that had already started to form. "My poor Olivia. I was so close to losing you."

She began to tremble. "I can't take much more, Gabe."

"Just hold on to me, my dearest," he said softly.

She grasped his upper arm with her hand and held on as he asked—for dear life. But beneath her fingers something was sticky and wet. She pulled her hand away. It was covered with blood.

"Gabe, it's a deep wound," she cried.

"Do not worry about it. We must leave, quickly. By now, the sheriff is tracking us, using his pack of hounds."

"We don't have to run anymore, Gabe. When the sheriff arrives, we can tell him what happened. Tancred admitted being the serial killer. He tried to kill me—and you! We can explain all that."

"Do you think the sheriff, my mortal enemy, is going to believe that Tancred is the killer? Why should he? For all Fremont knows, I could have asked Tancred for help and when he refused, I killed him. Or he could have found out I had murdered all those women and become a—what do you call it?"

"Serial killer."

"Yes, Tancred could have tried to capture me, and I killed him. There are so many possibilities, Olivia."

"But we have proof, Gabe. I'm a witness. I heard his confession."

He touched her face lightly, and when he replied, his words were sardonic. "Oh, yes, he would trust you, wouldn't he? The woman who helped me break out of jail. If I am innocent, why am I running, Olivia?"

"Because you've been set up. Framed."

"Framed." For a moment his face lost its tense look. "Another interesting use of the language, but, as you say, never mind. The crux of the matter is that the sheriff is hardly likely to take my word. And you are a criminal as well as I."

"Where can we go, Gabe?" she asked desperately.

"Where you suggested, Olivia. To America," he said simply, taking her hand. "We will head for the seacoast. One of the jewels will easily buy us passage."

Holding on to her arm, he led her through the house. He stopped at the front door and put out the candles. A faint sliver of moonlight reached them through the narrow windows as he took her in his arms.

"There is one more matter we must attend to. I want us to spend our future together as man and wife. I want to marry you, Olivia. Either here in England, aboard ship or in America. Wherever there is a man of the cloth to perform the ceremony. Will you be my bride?"

"Oh, yes, Gabe, yes! On land, sea or in the air, I'll be your bride."

He laughed as they went out the door. "In the air would be a little difficult, my dear."

"That's what you think."

They stepped into the night, where they were greeted by the sound of baying hounds. Gabriel tensed, listening.

"The sheriff's men and dogs. They have picked up our trail and are cutting us off from Eclipse. We will have to go on foot."

"Go where, Gabe?" she asked in near panic.

"Toward the stream beyond those hills. It is not very far away. We can mask our tracks in the water."

"Then let's hurry. The dogs are getting closer every moment."

LIV'S LUNGS were bursting for air. Her bruised throat was tight and each breath had become a painful gasp. The hills behind Barton Keep were steep and rocky, and traversing them in the dark was difficult and dangerous. More than once she fell, getting her foot wedged between two rocks or catching her clothes in tangled branches. They lost valuable minutes each time Gabe had to stop and help her.

Now she followed behind, trying to keep up. His shirt, gleaming white in the moonlight, was her beacon, but it became more and more difficult to follow as they trekked on and on. Where the hell was the stream he'd told her about? And even when they found it, how much farther would she have to walk before they were safe? They might never be safe, she realized as the hounds' barking continued and her aching muscles grew less responsive.

Gabe stopped, listening attentively, his head turned toward the sound of the dogs. "The hounds have not picked up our scent yet, but it will not be long." He pulled her close. "It is not so rough from here on," he assured her. "Just across the next field to the stream—"

"I need to rest," she begged. "Just for a minute."

She sank onto the damp grass, and Gabe dropped beside her, taking her in his arms. "I am so sorry, Olivia," he whispered, "that loving me has brought you such trouble—"

"And joy," she replied. "I never knew what it was to live so fully and love so completely until I met you." She kissed him tenderly. "I don't want to leave you, my darling, but if something happens to me, promise you'll go to America. Promise—"

"Nothing will happen to you, *that* is what I promise. We shall never be parted, and you will be my bride." His mouth closed hungrily on hers. "Somehow, across time, across space, in a way I shall never understand, we were brought together. It was meant to be. Written in the stars."

She felt the hot sting of tears in her eyes. Her heart overflowed with love for him in this night that had become the worst—and the best—night of her life. "Written in the stars," she repeated. "I believe that, too. It's the reason this has happened—so that we can be together despite all odds."

"And now the fates are with us again. A fog is settling in. Just hold on to me. We will reach the stream and then we go on toward the sea. And then—"

"America."

"Yes, my love." He pulled her to her feet. The fog swirled around them, much the same as it had that night she'd first met him. Full circle, she thought again. Only this time there was no magic book as her guide. She and Gabe had nothing but each other.

Even though he was only two steps ahead, Liv could barely see Gabe through the heavy mist. His hand was her lifeline. The baying of the dogs hadn't let up in spite of the mist. She was sure that she could hear the sound of men's voices carried on the wind.

Fighting exhaustion to keep up with him, she refused to think of capture. Or prison. Or life without Gabriel. But fear gripped her heart and as the fog enveloped them, she couldn't fight it off. They were on rough ground once more, filled with rocks and out-croppings. She tried to be careful, but Gabe was going too fast.

"Slow down," she cried, but her weak, feathery words barely penetrated the fog and he kept going, pulling her forward while she tried to hold on. The fog that hid them from their pursuers was not just thick but wet. Her fingers began to slip away from his grasp. Then she stumbled and fell, and her hand was wrenched from his.

"Gabriel," she cried, struggling to her feet. "Which way?"

"Here, Olivia. Over here!"

She plunged through the thick white haze, toward the sound of his voice. Her first step was on solid ground, the next on a rock, and then there was nothing but emptiness. She felt herself falling...

LIV AWOKE to faint strips of light filtering through the mist. She was lying on soft grass, her muscles aching, her clothing damp. She peered through the ghostly wisps. It was almost dawn, she realized, but the fog still swirled around her. She reached out, hoping to connect with Gabe, but he wasn't beside her. Panicked, she pushed herself up to a sitting position.

She was alone in the middle of nowhere. But what had happened to the dogs? Why hadn't the hounds found them? By this time, the sheriff and his men should have descended on them. But maybe they had!

When she fell, Gabe could have led their pursuers away from her. If that had happened, he could have been recaptured, even put back in jail. If the mob hadn't gotten to him first!

Near tears, Liv struggled to her feet just as the fog began to dissipate. It lifted in patches, revealing the surrounding landscape bit by bit, green and hilly with interspersed rocks that, she assumed, led to the stream. But it wasn't clear enough yet to see that far. She stood still as more and more was revealed.

Suddenly, her eyes widened in shock. She closed them, and then opened them rapidly. Her car was just a few yards away, tilted in a ditch. She was back in New York State!

Liv covered her face with her hands and moaned out loud. A dream? A coma? While she had been knocked out from the wreck, had she fantasized Gabriel?

"No, no," she said stubbornly. "He was real. He wasn't a dream." She touched her throat, and the bruises she felt there were validation of all that had happened. She swallowed hard. Her throat was raw and sore. "Thank God," she whispered, "it wasn't a dream."

Instinctively, her hand slid into her pocket. She pulled out a pair of ruby and sapphire earrings—further proof! Blood pulsed wildly through her veins. Her adventure had been real. She still wore the clothing of a servant from Northcliffe Manor. She had been to the eighteenth century and back. Alone. Gabriel wasn't with her.

Her thoughts were unbearable, but oddly logical. She'd come home, and Gabriel had been left behind. She clenched her hands into fists and raised them toward the clearing sky. "I can't bear it," she shouted. "I can't live without him. Gabriel, please be here!"

Behind her, over the hill, she heard a curse and then a familiar voice. "Must you shout, Olivia? There is a throbbing in my head as loud as a thunderstorm."

She raced through the haze, up the hill toward the sound of his voice. He was sitting on the ground, his head in his hands. She flew to him and flung her arms around his neck, knocking him flat. She covered his face with kisses.

"You're here, thank God. You're here with me! I thought I'd lost you."

"Of course I am here, Olivia." He sat up with her balanced precariously on top of his prone body. "Both of us must have taken a tumble over a cliff of some sort and escaped our pursuers. Let me see where we are."

She untangled herself from him and slowly they got to their feet. Gabe shook his head to clear it.

"You may be surprised, Gabe," she said quietly.

The fog had lifted completely and the sun shimmered in the eastern sky.

He glanced around. "I am surprised that Fremont and his dogs did not find us during the night."

"I think I know why." She took him by the hand. "Darling, this is going to be very difficult for you to believe, but we're not in England."

"Of course we are in England. You can tell by the greenness of the meadow and the scent of summer in the air." Nevertheless, a frown creased his forehead. "Although none of this looks familiar."

She led him to the top of the hill. "Look around, Gabe. We're in New York State. And the year is 1996."

"Olivia, Olivia," he chided. "Is there no end to your— My God, what the bloody hell is that?" He focused on the car in the ditch.

"That, my love, is my car. My automobile. The horseless carriage I told you about."

He rubbed his eyes. "I must have injured my head in the fall. Is this an illusion, Olivia?"

"Nope, you're seeing the real thing. Come closer and touch it."

He hesitated, but Olivia gave him a tug. "Come on. Closer. It won't bite."

"This automobile is like nothing I have ever seen..."

"A horse and carriage weren't all that familiar to me," she teased.

Gingerly, Gabriel touched the shiny surface of the car.

Liv shielded her eyes against the sun's reflection and peered inside. "There's the book—on the floorboard. If you help me open the door, I can reach in and get it."

Gabriel was willing to help, but she could tell that he didn't have the slightest idea how to open the car door.

"Push down on this part," she instructed, pointing toward the handle, "and then try to pull the door open. The accident has jammed it."

He managed to wrestle the door open and held on to her waist while she leaned in and snagged the book.

She held it up for him to see the title. "*Rogues Across Time*. And here you are," she said, finding the page and showing him the portrait.

His face mirrored his amazement. "Dear Lord, it *is* the portrait of me."

"A reproduction," she told him. "Read the last page—and find out all about yourself."

Gabriel's eyes darted along the paragraphs she pointed out. "The language is—"

"I know, a little different. But you understand it."

"Yes," he said, reading on, pausing, and then looking at her in confusion. "I thought you said that I was hanged in the year 1796."

"I did. You were, according to the book." Liv took it from him and read the lines he indicated, once and then again. Voice shaking, she repeated them aloud, "'Northcliffe escaped from jail and was pursued through the countryside. He eluded the sheriff and mysteriously vanished—'"

Her eyes widened with surprise as they met his. "I swear, it didn't say this before—"

"Read on," he urged.

"'To this day,'" she read, "'the fate of Gabriel Stratton, last Baron of Northcliffe, is unknown.'"

She closed the book and pressed it to her heart. The leather cover felt warm and comforting against her body. "We did it, Gabriel. We changed history."

He put his arm around her, but his hug was tentative. "I cannot understand any of this, Olivia. Where I am now . . . the story in the book . . ."

"It doesn't matter. We're together in our new home—America."

"How can I live in your world, in your time, Olivia? It is not possible." He shook his head vehemently.

"What's our choice, Gabe? If we go back, the sheriff will be waiting with the dogs," she said, unable to hide a smile. "We were coming to America, anyway. We just arrived in a different century."

"You are so calm about this, Olivia."

She gave him another hug. "Think about it, Gabe. This is the second time I've traveled through time. It's getting to be a habit." She caressed the soft leather of the book. "I was almost convinced that *this* made my impossible adventure possible, but now I know the answer—"

"God knows, I need answers," Gabe said fervently.

"It's not the book. It's our love, darling. You once said that a power greater than ourselves brought us together, and you were right. It's love, Gabe, the strongest force in the universe. Our love is powerful enough to move us through time and space and change history. Don't you see?"

"I know it must be true, but I am still confounded by all of this—and not sure what to do next." He closed his eyes for a moment and put his hand to his temple.

"We can go to the farm and dress your wounds," she said, noticing the dried blood around the gashes on his head and arm. "It's not Northcliffe Manor, Gabe, but it's a real home, a wonderful place for our children and our children's children to grow up. Here, just as in England, the land can be passed down from generation to generation."

She spoke hurriedly, not giving him a chance to interrupt. "And the stables you dreamed of are a real possibility. We can sell the earrings and buy your horses, the best in the state." She rushed on. "We'll restore my grandfather's stables and breed racehorses in a place where racing is still the sport of kings."

"But there is a problem, Olivia."

"I know. I'm going too fast. You have to think about all this. Maybe you don't want to stay in America. Well, you can return to England." Liv knew she was still talking a mile a minute, but she couldn't stop herself. There was so much to say. "It'll be modern England, but I suppose you'd be more at home there. And I'll go with you. I never thought of myself as an Anglophile, but who knows. Or you could—"

"Let me speak, Olivia. You *are* moving too quickly."

"I know. This is a terrible shock for you."

He raised a sardonic eyebrow. "A shock at the very least. And I need to put certain things in order."

She waited nervously.

"We must wed."

She breathed a sigh of relief. "Yes, my darling."

"We do not need to return to 'modern' England. It seems the fates have decreed that we will raise our family here in America." His voice was firm, his eyes determined, but he seemed more relaxed. "*Then* our horses. We will have the stables, Olivia, but you must promise me that you will learn to ride a little more expertly than you did on old Gracie."

"I promise, darling." For the first time, she saw the flicker of a smile curve his lips.

"Will you also promise to allow me time to get used to this new world?"

She kissed him tenderly. "All the time you need, but remember, this is our world now. I'll help you adapt to it."

"This *is* a miracle, my darling," he said softly. "Across time and space . . ."

"Our love is written in the stars," she completed for him.

He took her hand in his. The sun was warm on their faces, the breeze sweet with summer. "We face a new day, Olivia, in a new world."

"Together," she said softly, as they set out across the green fields toward home.

The leather book lay unnoticed in the grass where Liv had dropped it, its pages fluttering in the soft breeze.

Waiting . . .

HARLEQUIN® *Temptation*

MEN OF WHISKEY RIVER

Three sexy, unforgettable men
Three beautiful and *unusual* women

Come to Whiskey River, Arizona, a place "where anything can happen. And often does," says bestselling author JoAnn Ross of her new Temptation miniseries. "I envision Whiskey River as a romantic, magical place. A town like Brigadoon, hidden in the mists, just waiting to be discovered."

Enjoy three very *magical* romances.

#605 *Untamed* (Oct.)

#609 *Wanted!* (Nov.)

#613 *Ambushed* (Dec.)

Come and be spellbound

REBECCA
43 LIGHT STREET
YORK
FACE TO FACE

Bestselling author Rebecca York returns to "43 Light Street"
for an original story of past secrets, deadly deceptions—and
the most intimate betrayal.

She woke in a hospital—with amnesia…and with child.
According to her rescuer, whose striking face is the last
image she remembers, she's Justine Hollingsworth. But
nothing about her life seems to fit, except for the baby
inside her and Mike Lancer's arms around her. Consumed
by forbidden passion and racked by nameless fear, she
must discover if she is Justine…or the victim of some mind
game. Her life—and her unborn child's—depends on it.…

Don't miss *Face To Face*—Available in October, wherever
Harlequin books are sold.

HARLEQUIN ®

®

43FTF

Mail Order Men—Satisfaction Guaranteed!

Texas Man 3—*Travis Holt*

Running a ranch and raising three nieces is a real handful for this ex-rodeo champ, and he needs a good woman—fast.

Eve Reardon is willing to gamble on Travis if it means a secure home for her infant son. Love isn't part of the deal, but when their marriage of convenience becomes a passionate affair, Eve's heart is at stake. And Travis risks everything to win a nearly impossible prize: her trust.

#608 LUCK OF THE DRAW
by Candace Schuler

Available in October wherever
Harlequin books are sold.

When all the evidence points to love,
there's only one verdict.

VERDICT:
Matrimony

Witness the power of love this September as
seasoned courtroom lawyers discover that
sometimes there's just no defense against love.

This special collection of three complete stories
by your favorite authors makes a compelling
case for love.

WITHOUT PRECEDENT by JoAnn Ross
VOICES IN THE WIND by Sandra Canfield
A LEGAL AFFAIR by Bobby Hutchinson

Available this September wherever Harlequin
and Silhouette books are sold.

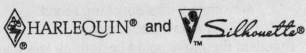 
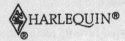 

Merry Christmas, Baby!

A romantic collection filled with the magic
of Christmas and the joy of children.

SUSAN WIGGS, Karen Young and
Bobby Hutchinson bring you Christmas wishes,
weddings and romance, in a charming
trio of stories that will warm up your
holiday season.

MERRY CHRISTMAS, BABY! also contains
Harlequin's special gift to you—a set of
FREE GIFT TAGS included in every book.

Brighten up your holiday season with
MERRY CHRISTMAS, BABY!

Available in November at
your favorite retail store.

HARLEQUIN®

Don't miss these Harlequin favorites by some of our most
distinguished authors!
And now, you can receive a discount by ordering two or more titles!

HT #25663	THE LAWMAN by Vicki Lewis Thompson	$3.25 U.S. ☐/$3.75 CAN.	☐
HP #11788	THE SISTER SWAP by Susan Napier	$3.25 U.S. ☐/$3.75 CAN.	☐
HR #03293	THE MAN WHO CAME FOR CHRISTMAS by Bethany Campbell	$2.99 U.S. ☐/$3.50 CAN.	☐
HS #70667	FATHERS & OTHER STRANGERS by Evelyn Crowe	$3.75 U.S. ☐/$4.25 CAN.	☐
HI #22198	MURDER BY THE BOOK by Margaret St. George	$2.89	☐
HAR #16520	THE ADVENTURESS by M.J. Rodgers	$3.50 U.S. ☐/$3.99 CAN.	☐
HH #28885	DESERT ROGUE by Erin Yorke	$4.50 U.S. ☐/$4.99 CAN.	☐

(limited quantities available on certain titles)

	AMOUNT	$
DEDUCT:	**10% DISCOUNT FOR 2+ BOOKS**	$
ADD:	**POSTAGE & HANDLING**	$
	($1.00 for one book, 50¢ for each additional)	
	APPLICABLE TAXES**	$ _____
	TOTAL PAYABLE	$ _____
	(check or money order—please do not send cash)	

To order, complete this form and send it, along with a check or money order for the
total above, payable to Harlequin Books, to: **In the U.S.:** 3010 Walden Avenue,
P.O. Box 9047, Buffalo, NY 14269-9047; **In Canada:** P.O. Box 613, Fort Erie, Ontario,
L2A 5X3.

Name:_____

Address:_____ City:_____

State/Prov.:_____ Zip/Postal Code:_____

**New York residents remit applicable sales taxes.
  Canadian residents remit applicable GST and provincial taxes. HBACK-JS3

Look us up on-line at: http://www.romance.net